I0627895

Look for More Titles by Cassandra Chandler

The Department of Homeworld Security

Gray Card
Resident Alien
Business or Pleasure
Tied up in Customs
Entry Visa
Duration of Stay
Duel Citizenship
Invasive Species
Export Duty
COALITION RECKONING
Import Quarantine
Homeworld for the Holidays
Nothing to Declare
Rate of Return
Trade Secrets
THE DEPARTMENT OF HOMEWORLD SECURITY OMNIBUS 1
THE DEPARTMENT OF HOMEWORLD SECURITY OMNIBUS 2

Cygnian 7

NUAR
KRAL
LAR
DORN

The Blades of Janus

PACK
PROGENITOR

The Forbidden Knights
FORBIDDEN INSTINCT

The Summer Park Psychics
WANDERING SOUL
WHISPERING HEARTS
LINGERING TOUCH
THE SUMMER PARK PSYCHICS OMNIBUS

Other Works
CRAFTING A WRITER'S LIFE: Building a Foundation

Coming Soon

The Blades of Janus
PERIHELION

Cygnian 7
BRON
TARN
ROM

Dorn: A Scifi Alien Warriors Romance

Cygnian 7
Book Four

Cassandra Chandler

Copyright Page

Dorn: A Scifi Alien Warriors Romance
Cygnian 7, Book Four

Print ISBN: 978-1-945702-93-8
Digital ISBN: 978-1-945702-92-1

First eBook edition: September 2022
First print edition: September 2022
10 9 8 7 6 5 4 3 2 1

cassandra-chandler.com
P.O. Box 91
Mission, Kansas 66201

Prologue

Wake up. Wake up. Please, wake up.

Amy shook her head sharply. Her living room was tilting at funhouse angles and making her stomach churn. She half expected the couch to slide across the carpet or the TV to topple over. That persistent voice was driving her crazy—unless she was already there. Insanity would explain the three men standing in front of her dressed in silver catsuits complete with broad belts and smooth chrome helmets covering the entirety of their heads.

Even in their bizarre 1950s sci-fi B movie costumes, the menace the enormous men exuded had her heart racing and her mouth bone dry. They were a threat to her and… someone else. Her head ached as she tried to remember. She wasn't alone, but she couldn't bring herself to look away from the danger in front of her. Instead, she brought more of her focus onto them, trying to sort out the muddle of thoughts fighting their way through.

Like time-delayed retina burn, the echo of a flash of light flooding the living room before the trio appeared and vaporized the sliding glass door seeped into her consciousness. How had they done that? She saw a distorted reflection of the room behind her in the gleaming, opaque faceplate of the intruder nearest her. In it, two distorted forms stood several feet away from her in the foyer—a man she didn't recognize grappling with a woman.

A woman... Sophie!

Amy's heart pounded in her chest so hard, splitting pain tore through her head. That's what Amy was trying to remember. Sophie was with her for sisters' movie night, but Becca, the eldest, had gone for a walk and wasn't there when the men broke in.

Wake up. Please wake up.

That voice again. It was so annoying, mostly because Amy couldn't ignore it. Something about it compelled her to listen—the deep baritone rumbling through her all the way to her bones and sending goosebumps racing over her skin.

Was this a dream? That would explain the vanishing glass and the silver-suited men. It didn't explain the terror that crept up her spine, tightening her throat until she could barely breathe. A nightmare, then. She was having a nightmare based on the last sci-fi movie binge-fest she'd shared with her family. It hadn't been too long ago. All Amy had to do was wake up and this would all be over.

It would all be over…

A sharp pain pierced her shoulder. She tried to reach

over and grab the spot, but both arms stayed immobile. Shit, it was one of those dreams where she couldn't move. She had never felt pain in a dream before. Her left shoulder throbbed and ached.

The intruder at the front of the group lifted his arm and time slowed. Behind him, one of the other silver-suited men lurched forward, his arms outstretched as he reached for the man standing before her. Amy had to stop them. Sophie stood behind her, and something bad was about to happen. Amy flung herself forward. She felt the pull of gravity as she leapt, finally able to move, though it was like pushing through molasses.

Part of her wanted to laugh at the absurdity of it. Her heart pounded too hard to let her, her skin was electrified with warning. This was real. It might be a dream, but it was also real somehow. A memory.

The silver-suited intruder at the front of the group hit a button on the high-tech bracer that covered his right forearm. The man behind him grabbed him too late. A sharp ray of blinding light erupted from the bracer, flying out into the room toward Amy. She watched it approach, knowing nothing she could do would stop it, praying that it wouldn't hit Sophie as well.

This was going to hurt. Amy's shoulder burned and her back throbbed as though someone had beaten her with a bat all up and down its length. The blinding white light came nearer—almost touching her skin.

Wake up. Please. I need you with me.

The disembodied man's voice tugged at her heart. She wanted to be with him, whoever he was. A desperate longing rose within her to see his face, to touch the lips that called to her so plaintively. She wanted him to wrap his arms around her and keep her safe.

The moment the blast hit her shoulder, a soothing green light appeared all over her body and the energy fizzled out harmlessly. The men before her stepped back, heads turning side to side as if confused, then they vanished, too.

The glow intensified. It swept over her, a loving caress that made the pain disappear, soaking into her muscles and bones, soothing her. Her skin rose in gooseflesh and her heart pounded for an entirely new reason. A current of electricity flowed down her spine, quickening her breath and sending energy coursing along her limbs. Desire pooled in her belly, her face tingled, and a molten heat flooded her body.

What was going on? She'd never had a dream like this before. Everything was so vivid, so real. But this wasn't a memory. Not yet, anyway.

Amy. Come back to me. Wake up. I need you.

She opened her eyes.

Chapter One

Amy stared up at a smooth white ceiling. Odd fragments of rainbows were flickering in her blurred vision. Her mouth felt as if she'd been drinking sandpaper smoothies, and her head spun from the images of the strange memory-dream. Someone had taken her from her home. Men dressed up as characters straight out of a low budget sci-fi movie had attacked Amy and her sister, Sophie. Except they hadn't just been doing some kind of cosplay. They'd carried weapons. *Actual* weapons, capable of doing things no technology she knew of could do. No technology from Earth.

Was she seriously considering this? That aliens had abducted her?

Her heart raced, pounding against her chest in a punishing beat. Whatever was happening, if she was going to get herself and Sophie out of this, Amy needed to control her emotions and think clearly—to calm down and assess her environment and situation. Sophie would be helpless. It was up to Amy to save them.

Her left shoulder was strangely stiff and a constant

current ran up and down her spine. The not-unpleasant tingling spread over her back and down her arms and legs. She twitched her fingers and toes unobtrusively to make sure she could move while taking in more details about her surroundings.

There were no tiles or overhead lights, though the room was brightly lit. She blinked repeatedly to bring her view into focus. The wall above her head was also white, with a monitor built into it, integrated so seamlessly that she couldn't see a gap around the edges of the screen. Various shapes in different colors pulsed, spiked, or faded in and out on its otherwise black surface. She had never seen a vitals display like it, but she would bet she was in some kind of hospital.

A wave of shivers passed through her like the ones she would get when she'd been sick for a while and hadn't moved enough, but the stiffness in her shoulder warned her away from trying to rise. The shivers turned to tingling, the hair on her arms and legs standing on end and her spine becoming a racetrack for arcs like lightning along her nerves. What the hell was that? She blinked a few times to clear her vision, her eyes drawn to her left. Her heart picked up again, pounding against her chest as the tingling in her spine and skin intensified a hundredfold.

A man was standing near her bed. Or at least, a male… something. He looked mostly human, but his skin was the pale blue of a perfect spring sky. His eyes glowed vibrant green, the color so intense, it tinged his high cheekbones and strong brow. His hair was white, flowing around his shoulders, but with the bangs pulled back in a ponytail. Her 'abducted-by-aliens' theory was definitely gaining credibility.

From where she lay, he seemed impossibly tall. He must be pushing seven feet, if not more. Cords of muscles stood out on his arms, shoulders and jaw. His cheekbones were chiseled perfection. The tight, white leather pants he wore clung to muscular thighs thicker than her waist. He wore a sleeveless tunic of matching material that laced up the front, giving her a tantalizing view of sculpted abs and a chest she wanted to turn into a cheese tray.

Was she still dreaming? This guy was too gorgeous to be real, her reaction to him too visceral. Her hands curled, the skin of her fingertips tingling and her palms itching with the desire to touch him. She would pull his hair loose and run her fingers through it, then figure out how to untie those laces on his shirt as she kissed the curve of his lips. The curve that was deepening as he smirked at her as if he was privy to some secret that amused him.

His smile hit her like a nuke going off in her nether regions. More of her skin broke out in goosebumps. Stiff shoulder or not, she wanted to get up and throw herself at him. She mercilessly clamped down on the urge.

What the hell was going on? Had someone drugged her? Her mind was clear, though. Then again, drugs would explain the pale rainbows she was still seeing floating in the air, especially around the blue giant. They faded the longer she stared at him.

She must still be dreaming. Or maybe hallucinating. Except the weirdness started long before waking up here—back at her house when those three guys showed up in silver catsuits and shot her with a ray-beam. Her heart picked up at the memory, her chest tightening as the recent fear came back full force. The giant's pale white eyebrows pulled together, the corners of his eyes pinched with concern. The emotion emanated from him like a palpable thing—yet another form of hallucination? He reached for her with his huge hand, fingers outstretched. The tips of his nails were sharp like claws.

Somehow, she knew his touch would be gentle, his hands strong and warm. He would hold her close and protect her. No one would ever hurt her again. The pull toward him was so strong, her entire body tingled with it. Her core tightened and wave after wave of goosebumps spread across her skin. If she let herself fall toward him, into him, they would share a bliss unlike anything she'd ever experienced. All she had to do was let go.

Right before his hand touched her shoulder, she flung herself to the side, rolling off the bed and landing in a crouch. She leapt back, needing more space to maneuver, and ended up in a fighting stance, feet set wide, her arms up and ready to defend herself. The light in the room caught and reflected off of two shimmering wristbands made of a substance that gleamed like chrome, but with some kind of transparent crystal-like material coating it. Lights of every color dotted their surface in a complex pattern that made no sense. Her eyebrows lifted as she quickly looked them over, trying to find a hinge or a keyhole or any way to remove them. There wasn't so much as a seam where someone had welded them together on her forearms.

"Amy."

The blue giant's familiar voice coursed through her like the vibration of a plucked guitar string, starting in her feet and thrumming its way all up through her body. The same voice as in her dream. A jolt of energy seared her spine, electric arcs of pleasure zinging along her arms and legs. She didn't know her name could sound so sensual, so full of need. Ever so briefly, she closed her eyes, fighting off the sensations, trying to tamp them down. She finally gave up, settling instead on ignoring them and glaring at the threat before her.

She swallowed hard. "And you are?"

His perfect lips quirked up in a half-smile that sent more heat pulsing through her. In that low, rumbling voice, he said, "Dorn."

"Just Dorn? No last name?"

"Dorn is the first, last, and only name I was given."

"Fair enough. Speaking of gifts, care to tell me about

these fancy handcuffs?"

His brow furrowed, and his smirk faded. "Those are wristbands, not handcuffs."

"Potato, po-tah-to."

He cocked his head to the side, brow slightly furrowed. They probably didn't have potatoes where he was from.

"If they aren't cuffs, then tell me how to take them off," she said.

"You need to wear them for your protection. They're a gift, not a means to control you."

"Can you use them to control me?"

His lips parted briefly, then he snapped his mouth shut.

She snorted. "And there's my answer."

Dorn stepped around the bed, and she backed away further. Damn, he was huge. She had felt better when there was at least something between them—a bit of cover for her to hide behind when this situation inevitably went pear-shaped. As he lifted his hands, she noticed he was wearing wristbands that looked exactly like hers. Briefly, she wondered if he was in the same mess that she was. They could band together and fight off the bad guys, rescue Sophie, and escape back to Earth, where Amy would show him her appreciation by—

She shook herself, forcing her attention back to the reality of her unbelievable situation. That was a complete fantasy. She wasn't a daydreaming romantic like Sophie, who fell for any hot guy that caught her eye. Wait…

Amy glanced back at Dorn's wristbands. She had seen something similar recently. A friend of their older brother, Buddy, had crashed family dinner only a few days ago. Kral. He was as tall as Dorn and even more thickly muscled—and he'd worn the same style of wristbands, only without the flashy colors. Kral hadn't been blue, but who knew what these guys could do with their advanced technology.

Her stomach tightened as she realized Becca might be in as much danger as Amy and Sophie. Kral had been extremely focused on their eldest sister. But he was a friend of Buddy's, and Buddy was extremely overprotective of them all—especially Amy. He wouldn't bring someone dangerous into their lives. Then again, Kral's presence had agitated Buddy. He was desperate for Kral to leave. There was more going on with that dynamic than Amy could sort out at the moment.

She couldn't make decisions based on hopeful speculation. No. Dorn knew what was going on and was part of it. Amy's family was in danger. She needed to see him as an enemy, not a potential date. Whatever he did to make her want him so much, she needed to fight it with everything she had.

Chapter Two

This wasn't going well. Here was his soulmate, standing right before him, and the strongest emotion she was exuding was mistrust. There was plenty of arousal wrapped around it, but at her core, she didn't trust him. She saw him as a threat. Amy was supposed to know him instinctively. He carried the other half of her soul. His hearts clenched at the thought that something might be wrong with their bond. How could she not feel their connection?

He wanted to pace the length of the room, or simply grab her and kiss her until she recognized what he was to her, but after everything he'd learned watching his fellow Cygnian warriors courting their human females, he knew better than to push her too quickly. Instead, he held himself in check and studied her, desperate to figure out a way to reach her.

She stood before him in a fighting stance, feet planted wide and ready to carry her in any direction, arms up and prepared to defend herself. He sensed no fear from her, just a calm determination and something… familiar. A piercing desire to protect those dear to her. The emotion was one he'd experienced so often, it took him a moment to separate his own feelings from hers. Though her body betrayed no movement, he could see the spark in her eyes as she assessed him, looking for weaknesses and planning her attack.

A thrill shot through him as he realized just how perfect she was for him. He was in charge of security for his prism, the group of Cygnian warriors whose souls shared a special bond of brotherhood. His was a rare full prism, with seven members, including Kral, the Crown Prince of Cygnus-Prime.

Though most Cygnians thought of themselves as invulnerable, Dorn knew better than most that his people were not immune to harm. Even before what had happened to his other prism-mate, Lar, Dorn knew. Security specialists were seen as more of a ceremonial position in their society than a functional one. If they hadn't been, perhaps his birth brother wouldn't have had to go through his childhood ordeal.

"What are you?" Amy's sharp tone pulled him back from his dark thoughts.

"I am a Cygnian warrior," Dorn said, pride flooding his chest as it always did.

"What can you do?"

He angled his head, trying to sort out the intent behind her question. "I can do anything a human male can." He took a step forward, but she retreated again, her feet moving in an odd, smooth gait. Her arms rose a bit higher and her lips tightened into a thin line.

She narrowed her eyes, and said, "Can you swim?"

Maker. How did she know he couldn't swim? He knew she was looking for weaknesses, but did she expect him to just tell her? He would gladly share anything about himself that she wanted to know if it brought them closer together, but he didn't like the thought of her assuming that other alien sentients she met might be so forthcoming.

"I suppose I can do *most* of the things a human male can," he said. "And many more."

He smirked as he focused on the electric arcs of pleasure firing along his spine plates, knowing that, as his soulmate, she had to be feeling something similar. If what the other warriors in his prism had told him was true, focusing on the sensation would amplify what she was experiencing, adding his pleasure to her own. She gasped, brown eyes widening and lush lips parting. Her cheeks and neck flushed and her heart accelerated, his dual, discordant beats quickening in an attempt to match hers.

She shook her head and said, "Stop that."

"Stop what?" He took another step forward and this time she didn't retreat.

"Stop putting your alien pheromone whammy on me."

"'Alien pheromone whammy?' I have no idea what that is."

"Bullshit," she said. "If you didn't know what I'm talking about, you wouldn't look so smug."

His grin broadened. Nothing slipped past his soulmate.

"How did you know I can't swim?" he asked.

"Lucky guess. You're deflecting."

"Deflecting. That's an interesting word." He nodded, overplaying his pondering. "It implies warding something off. Turning away an attack." He stepped closer again, till he could almost feel her heat. Leaning in a bit, he said, "Are we sparring, Amy?"

Her eyes narrowed further. He would love nothing more than to answer the challenge in her gaze, though melee with one's soulmate carried a much more significant meaning for his people. He wasn't certain if he should indulge her, tempting as it was.

The shoulder where she had been shot was fully healed, but scans revealed there was an unusual tightening of the ligaments and tendons of that entire side of her chest, along with her left shoulder, arm, and back. The medics aboard the space station, *Outreach*, where Dorn had brought Amy after they realized there was an issue, thought it might be a side-effect of the Cygnian healing technology used to tend her wounds shortly after they had occurred, but they were still gathering data.

Dorn's hearts beat faster as he remembered how he had first seen Amy, lying on the floor of her home in a pile of books, her shoulder a charred mess of burnt tissue. She had barely been alive, the blood loss and internal damage she'd sustained severe enough to require several days in their healing chamber.

The moment he had touched her, his pity and fascination turned to shock and then terror. He had instantly known that she was his soulmate—his one chance in this lifetime to be whole. Perhaps she needed to touch him to recognize their connection as well. Accepting her challenge became even more tempting. But before he did anything else, he needed to reassure her that she was safe.

"I won't hurt you," Dorn said. "No one here will."

Amy barely kept herself from laughing again. "As long as I keep on the control bracelets."

"They aren't control bracelets."

His frustration rolled off of him, crashing into her and making her heart pick up again. She took a deep breath and blew it out as surreptitiously as she could. He did the same, though he wasn't trying to mask his efforts at regulating his emotions.

"Those are Cygnian wristbands," he said. "They are a highly coveted gift containing our incredibly advanced technology."

She didn't doubt it. The men in silver catsuits had worn

bracers on their forearms that they used to vaporize her sliding glass door and burn a hole through her body. She winced at the memory, flexing her shoulder slightly to test the injury. No pain accompanied the movement, but that odd tightness was still there. It spread down her back across her shoulder blade and through the muscles beneath her left breast as well. The injury seemed to be healed, but the muscles and tendons were still zinging from it.

"So, what can they do?" She didn't figure he'd tell her, but didn't see the harm in asking since he was trying to paint the 'gift' in such a rosy light. "Deflect bullets? Change my outfit if I spin around in a circle a bunch of times?"

One of his eyebrows arched. "Spinning isn't involved, but they can create shielding that will deflect all kinds of weapons fire. They can also create holoprojections that alter one's appearance."

He struck his wristbands together, creating a lingering chime that sounded like a tuning fork at first, but grew louder, the sustained note reminding her of Tibetan singing bowls. A low, rumbling hum joined in, the deep sound penetrating her muscles and making her bones vibrate in the most pleasurable way. It was like getting an erotic massage from the inside-out. Her lungs sucked in air, her heart pounded, and her core clenched yet again.

"What…" She licked her lips and shook her head. "What are you doing?"

"Activating the vocal controls."

A shimmer passed over his body. She blinked, uncertain of her senses again. The man before her looked like a regular guy. Okay, maybe not regular. He was still over seven feet tall and packed with muscle, but aside from the gleam in his green eyes, he just looked like a guy from Earth. An incredibly hot, kinda pale guy with white hair. His smirk returned and his eyes narrowed as he watched her ogling him. She had to get it together and *keep* it together.

So, that was how Kral had looked like an Earthling for their family dinner. The holoprojection hadn't been able to cover up for his odd conversation or him letting things slip like not being able to swim.

"Great," she said, letting her tone drip with sarcasm. "I can turn myself blue with these things. That sounds really great for my safety."

Dorn laughed, a throaty, rich sound that set her off again. She was starting to get used to it, though. A wave of pleasure thrummed through her body, but she let it pass, keeping herself as detached from it as she could.

Who the hell was she kidding? His laugh was so hot, it could melt butter. He hummed another note while she struggled with her composure and the illusion vanished. Her heartbeat picked up again and her mouth went dry. Shit, she actually liked him better this way. What was wrong with her? His smirk returned full-force, but thankfully he kept himself on topic.

"A specific note will create shields against weapons," he said. "Another makes atmospheric shielding that protects you from the radiation and the vacuum of space. It even creates a thin pocket of air for you to breathe, as long as the power lasts."

"Handy." She couldn't believe how open he was being. Still, she doubted he would give her a music lesson in all the notes and tones needed to control the damn things. "What if you don't have enough air in your lungs to make the necessary sound to activate those controls in the first place?"

His eyes widened and a feeling of pride swept through her. Where the hell was that coming from? Him? But why would that make him proud and how could she be feeling his emotions? Maybe she hadn't been drugged but was succumbing to some kind of alien pheromones. She hadn't been entirely serious when she mentioned it before, but now she wondered if he really was affecting her that way.

Just the thought of it made her profoundly uncomfortable. She did not want to be getting up in his business. Okay, part of her did, but it was a stupid part. A part that didn't think about the quid-pro-quo. What if he could feel her emotions, too? She cringed at the thought of how many times she'd been nearly overwhelmed by her attraction to him.

"There are touch commands as well," he said. "They're

color coded, but at a wavelength that humans can't perceive."

Amy's gaze flitted to the very colorful wristbands she still held up in front of her chest, arms readied to fight or defend. Humans couldn't perceive them? Great. Let him keep thinking that.

"Humor me," she said. "What color for the atmospheric shielding?"

"Gold," he said. "Like the color of the shield itself. Blue for the defensive shielding. It can be used to create a small shield on our forearm or projected to protect targets near us. White is for the blaster function," he added, almost as an afterthought.

She noted the location of each button as he listed them, repeating them in her mind over and over and committing them to memory. The white control wasn't just a button but a long panel. If she had to guess, she would say that was a power-up dial. She really hoped she wouldn't have to put that guess into practice.

"Communicator?" she asked.

"Green, but it needs additional commands to connect to your intended recipient."

That made sense. She wanted him to think this was idle curiosity, so she said, "Holoprojector?" next.

Again, pride washed over her. Did he think she wasn't paying attention when he talked about it earlier?

"Pale blue," he said, "but again, it needs quite a bit of

setup to create the appearance you desire."

"Could I make myself look like a totally different person, or does it only make minor changes?"

Unease rippled out to her. Why would that question unsettle him?

"You could use it to look like a very different person, but they would still have the same dimensions as you," he said. "It can't make you taller or shorter and it can't cover certain physical characteristics that extend beyond the form you're emulating."

"What?"

That had her shaking her head. She couldn't quite picture what he was talking about until he half-turned, revealing rows of tall… fins or something protruding from the center of his back. They were smaller below his neck and at the base of his spine, rising up to maybe ten inches at their highest at the midpoint. As she watched, the pins between the membranes connecting them began to ripple, faster and faster, till the fins blurred, like a hummingbird's wings. She felt their vibration through the air, a tremor that pulsed through her muscles and deep into her bones, sparking more of that incredible pleasure.

The skin above her spine was practically on fire from the current running up and down its length. Heat built between her legs, her core clenched with an aching need to wrap around him. Her hands itched to explore him, to find more of his alien features and the spots that would have him melting as much as he was melting her. Her eyes had to be bugging from her head. She shook herself and snapped her gaping mouth shut. Everything about this guy drew her in. It didn't help that she had probably read a thousand sci-fi romances and Dorn hit all the right buttons for her.

She was supposed to be thinking about her sister. How to rescue Sophie. How to find this guy's weaknesses so Amy could escape. She needed to be thinking of how to take him down, not… how to 'take him down.' Shaking herself again, she tried to clear her mind and focus. She couldn't let him tempt her.

Chapter Three

"What..." Amy's voice came out low and raspy, surprising her. She coughed to clear it, then said, "What are those?"

Dorn's smirk returned. "Spine plates. Cygnians have certain... anatomical differences from humans."

Her mind immediately presented all kinds of possibilities that had her nearly reeling. She had to pull herself together. Sophie was counting on her. Amy was their only chance at escape. She didn't have time to be fantasizing over a giant, gorgeous alien who might have some very interesting... differences... in his anatomy.

Again, she cleared her throat, then said, "Am I free to go?"

His lips thinned into a tight line, and he shook his head. At least he was being honest.

"You're on a space station," he said. "Leaving would be... problematic."

Amy let out a short laugh. "For whom?"

"For lots of people, including you and your family."

Her veins felt as though they flooded with ice. Were

they after more than just her sisters? How much danger were they in?

A vague memory tried to form in her mind. There had been more than three men in her house. The fourth… The fourth hadn't really been a man at all. He was the one who had taken Sophie. Somehow, she knew that the fourth man wasn't Dorn, but that didn't mean he wasn't working with the whole group. She couldn't let her reaction to Dorn get in the way of reason. Not when he was talking about her family.

"Don't you dare bring my family into this," Amy said.

"Your family is already involved. Your sister Becca is with our Crown Prince."

Shit, they had Becca, too? All that left was Buddy, and they'd have all of her siblings. Except Hayley, her honorary sister. For the first time, Amy was glad they weren't blood relatives. Maybe it would keep her safe and out of this mess.

"We need to keep you and Sophie close," Dorn said.

Amy's heart fell. They *did* have Sophie. He had confirmed all of Amy's worst fears. And now it was up to her to save them all.

"So, I'm not free to go," she said.

Dorn shrugged, then shook his head.

Amy nodded as she stepped away from him, needing a bit more space to do something, anything to get herself out of this. She kept her emotions as level as she could, just in case he was reading her. She needed every advantage she could get

"Okay, then," she said. She quickly lifted her right arm, keeping her hand in a fist and pointing it at Dorn as she slid her finger along the white line on her wristband. A bolt of white light shot out of it, momentarily bright enough to blind her.

Dorn barely managed to dodge Amy's attack, humming notes to activate his personal shielding as he twisted his body out of the way. The blast hit the wall behind him, leaving a large scorch mark across the gleaming surface. Thank the goddess it hadn't hit the viewport. The transparent material wasn't as sturdy as the hull. He activated the blue shield on his left arm, making a point of letting her see it and that he was ready should she fire again.

She, of all sentients, shouldn't have been able to surprise him. He knew that she was agitated, but he hadn't sensed the change in her mind, the decision to act on it. She was as skilled at masking her intentions and emotions as he was.

"Don't do that again," he said.

"Or what?" She slowly circled him, arms at her sides in mock relaxation. He could sense how her body was actually coiled, ready to strike at any moment. “You’ll take me prisoner?”

“You aren’t my prisoner.”

“Then what am I?”

He took a deep breath, then let it out. “My soulmate.”

She paused in her stalking him like prey, her eyebrows arching up her forehead and her mouth dropping open. Her lips pulled into a smirk and she laughed.

“Right,” she said, drawing out the word.

“It’s true.” He took a step forward, something about her tone compelling him to try to convince her. She lurched back, her frown returning. In a calmer voice, he said, “I carry the other half of your soul. You must sense it. There is no ‘alien pheromone whammy.’ Your soul recognizes mine.”

Her lips tightened, but the edges pulled up. Was she laughing at him? How could she find this concept so ludicrous? Frustration tightened his chest.

“Soulmates are real,” he said.

“Fine.” She waved her hands dismissively, which only increased his ire. “Then you should be trying to help me.”

“I am.”

“Okay, then take me to my sister.”

“That was always the plan,” he said, his voice harsher than he’d intended. “She is on our ship within Ceres.”

“Ceres?” Amy’s brow furrowed.

“It’s a dwarf planet in your asteroid belt.”

"So, we're still close to Earth."

"Of course. We wouldn't take you far from your homes, especially since some of our group haven't found their soulmates yet."

She frowned, a wave of anger was rolling out from her. "And these soulmates are more women from Earth that you plan to take to your ship."

"If they wish." He sighed again. "You make it sound as though we are taking them against their will. We aren't."

"Except for me, who can't leave the station."

"You were injured."

"I was attacked," she yelled. For the first time, a trace of fear leaked out to him. "I was *taken*."

He wanted to wrap his arms around her, to tell her that he would keep her safe and no one would ever hurt her again. From the murderous look in her eyes, he knew that would not be welcome. He would be the one who needed protection should he try.

"We only took you to heal you," Dorn said. "You would have died if we had left you as we found you." His stomach felt as though it turned to ice at the thought. He let his terror seep through to her, wanting her to know how it had pained him to lift her bloodied body from the floor of her dwelling, how he had watched over her, willing her to fight, to hold on to life as she healed.

Her eyes widened only slightly, a wave of apprehension flowing from her, before she steeled herself and said,

"Well, I seem fine now, so why don't you return my sisters and me to Earth?"

"Because they don't want to go back. They want to stay with their soulmates."

An odd shiver coated his skin at the cold gleam that filled her eyes. Her upper lip curled briefly, and she settled back into a warrior's stance, her arms rising.

"You've twisted their minds," Amy said. "It won't work on me."

"We have twisted nothing. The soulmate bond is a gift. It is the most sacred and beautiful aspect of our existence."

"Good for you. Just leave us out of it."

His exasperation blew out of him in a gusty breath. "How can we when you are the ones who hold the other halves of our souls?"

"My soul is mine."

"Yes. And mine is also yours. We are one."

She rolled her eyes and made a rude, dismissive noise. His frustration turned to anger. He knew she could sense their connection, even if she didn't understand it. But to speak so ill of the soulmate bond, to disrespect it so completely was driving him crazy. Without thinking, he lifted his left arm, holding his shield higher, his right hand curling into a fist. Amy's eyes widened briefly as she took in the challenge in his posture. She raised her own arms, quickly tapping on her left wristband to activate her shielding.

How was she doing that? Humans shouldn't be able to see the controls on Cygnian wristbands. The healing from their medical chamber had affected her strangely, but it had only addressed her injuries and none were near her eyes or optical receptors. Dorn thought back over everything that had happened since she'd been in his care. There had been so many extraordinary events, even a bizarre interaction with their goddess, the Cygnian Maker.

Wait… Sophie and Lar had fought the Maker to save him from death. During the battle, the Maker had sent energy coursing through every member of their prism as well as the human soulmates who were present. Dorn had thought Amy was unaffected since she had been in stasis when it happened. Perhaps he was wrong.

Sophie had been altered radically, given powers they didn't understand, and Lar's spine plates were now infused with lightning. The Maker had told Lar that she was changing them so that they would be more compatible with their human soulmates. What if she had altered Amy more than any of them realized?

"Amy, I think we need the healers to take another look at you," he said.

"Take another step toward me, and you're the one who's going to need a healer."

A mix of pride and concern flooded him. His mate was beyond fierce. She was ferocious. He needed to find some common ground for them to meet on, a more familiar frame for her to see their situation. How could he help her understand that he was on her side when she kept challenging him? Unless… Unless the challenge was the key to bridging the gap between them.

Dorn hummed the note that would activate his wristbands' communications channel, then another to connect him with Kral. In moments, his Crown Prince appeared through the holoprojectors that had been built into the station's medical bay. Kral's sapphire skin gleamed in the light, his dark blue hair billowing about his face in a wild mane matched by his beard. Even as a projection, his presence filled the room, and not just because of his enormous stature.

Outreach station had partnered with Dorn's prism and had integrated Cygnian technology into their holoprojection systems. Kral looked as real and solid as Amy, though Dorn could sense that he wasn't truly there through their prism bond. Kral's eyes widened, gleaming orange as he stared at Amy. She looked equally as surprised to see him.

"Amy," Kral said. "I'm glad to see you up and… well." His voice trailed off as he took in the active shield on her arm, along with her stance and expression. He turned to Dorn, one eyebrow arched in inquiry.

"We're having some issues with our interactions," Dorn said.

"Kral?" Amy asked.

"A holoprojection of him," Dorn said.

Kral smiled at her. "I'm pleased you recognize me."

"You're Buddy's friend," Amy's lips thinned, mistrust rolling off of her like thunderclouds. "Does he know you're an alien?"

"Buddy knows about all of us," Dorn said.

The mistrust hovering around her was spiked with a strong dose of betrayal. Dorn needed to stop this before it went any farther. He needed to find a way to get through to her.

"It seems our challenge is happening faster than anticipated," Dorn said, turning to Kral.

Kral's eyes widened with surprise. "A challenge? Already? None of us have challenged our soulmates, and we've even claimed them."

A sharp spike of anxiety shot out from Amy, followed by rage. Dorn could somewhat understand that she didn't believe in soulmates, but why would the thought of her sisters bonding with Cygnians make her so upset? Unless she took issue with them being with aliens. Dorn couldn't bear the thought. He had to find a way to win her over. He couldn't lose her. If she only spent time with her sisters and their mates, she would come to understand the deep and eternal love that soulmates shared. He knew he could make her happier than any other sentient in the universe—otherwise he would step aside.

"Our path is different," Dorn said.

Kral turned to Amy. "You understand the meaning of the challenge? When Dorn challenges you and wins, you will be his—"

"*If* he wins," Amy quickly interrupted. "What if he loses?"

Kral shrugged. "Then nothing changes."

"And what if I challenge him and win?" she asked. "Is he mine then?"

Kral smiled and nodded. "Yes, but—"

"Then I challenge him." She shifted her weight back and forth, standing straighter. "Right here, right now."

"Amy," Dorn chided. "You have no hope of beating me."

"Then you have nothing to be worried about," she said.

Dorn's plan was blowing up in his face. If he had issued the challenge first, he could quickly subdue her. In any challenge, he had to fight her with all he had, and there was no way she could defeat him. She might hurt herself trying.

"I need to be the one to challenge you," Dorn said.

"Too late," she snapped. "Do you accept my challenge or not?"

Dorn looked to Kral, but his leader, his friend, simply shook his head. They both knew there was no way around this.

Dorn sighed heavily, then said, "I do."

Chapter Four

What the hell was she doing? Amy was so angry, her hands shook. She had to be crazy, challenging this alien warrior who was twice her size. Dorn was right about her odds of beating him. Still, if there was any chance that she could get the upper hand in their relationship by defeating him—or, hell, incapacitate him long enough to escape—she had to try. From the sound of it, she wouldn't be any worse off if she lost, plus then he wouldn't 'win her' in battle.

Just the thought of it was enough to make her really want to kick his ass. Kral said the Cygnians holding Sophie and Becca hadn't done this challenge thing, but they had 'claimed' them. Bile rose in Amy's throat as she thought about what that could mean. Becca had seemed really into Kral when he'd crashed their family dinner, but it was way too fast for her stoic older sister to be hopping into the sack with someone—especially someone from another planet.

Amy shook her head forcefully, refusing to let her mind go through many possibilities there. If she thought about what they might mean by 'claiming,' what her sisters might be going through, she would become too emotional and she'd have no chance of beating Dorn. Amy couldn't overpower him, so she needed to outsmart him.

Kral stared at her for a few long moments, then lifted his arm and started tapping on various spots of his own wristbands. "Very well," he said. "I have officially logged your challenge and will stand as witness. You may begin when—"

Amy didn't wait for him to finish. She fired a blast at Dorn. He crouched low, easily raising his shield in time to absorb the energy from her wristband.

"Shields first," he yelled, a mix of fear and frustration hitting her.

He wasn't afraid of losing. It was more fear *for* her than *of* her. Under different circumstances, if she could trust him or knew he wasn't trying to manipulate her emotions, she might have been touched by his concern. This was her reality, though. He could be purposefully feeding her whatever emotions he wanted to get her to let down her guard. For all she knew, everything she felt from him was a ruse meant to win her sympathy. She would never let that happen.

"I already have a shield," she said.

"Atmospheric and personal protection shielding," Dorn said. "I won't risk you being hurt again."

She rolled her eyes, but tapped on the golden light on

her wristband. A field in the same color flowed out from them both, coating her entire body.

"Happy?" she asked, pushing as much snark into her tone as she could.

Dorn grumbled something, then said, "Hit the orange buttons as well. They'll enhance your strength."

She arched an eyebrow at him, wondering whether to trust him or not. "Are you turning yours on, too?"

"I'm trying to give you as many advantages as I can," he said. "If we're going to do this, we're going to do it right."

"So, it'll make me as strong as you?"

He laughed. "No. But it'll at least make you a little closer."

Damn his cocky attitude. She wanted to kick his ass even more. Someone needed to teach him a lesson, and she was the only one in the room. She tapped the orange button on both wristbands. The gold field surrounding her flickered for a moment, but aside from that, she didn't notice anything different.

The skin on the nape of her neck rose in gooseflesh, and she ducked instinctively. Dorn had lashed out, trying to grapple her. Amy coiled her body, dropping low and sinking her energy into the balls of her feet. She launched up, landing a series of punches along the bottom of his rib cage. The blows landed much harder than she expected, especially the ones from her left arm. She drew it back and slammed the heel of her palm into his solar plexus as hard as she could. His green eyes widened in shock as he flew back several paces, stumbling to keep his balance.

She couldn't give him a chance to catch his breath. She had taken him off guard and needed to keep him there. Pursuing, she followed, kicking at his knees to try to make his legs buckle. It was about as effective as kicking a fire hydrant. His equilibrium restored, he swung at her again. She lifted her shield in time to block the blow, but the impact still sent a shockwave through her left arm and shoulder. This time, she was the one who staggered back.

"Are you alright?" he asked, the concern flowing out from him almost enough to make her hesitate. "Your shoulder…"

He dropped his guard, leaning over her left side as he looked at her shoulder. He should have been watching her elbow.

Using one of the less mainstream martial arts that she'd studied, she brought her elbow up under his chin hard enough that his head snapped back. His arms flailed at his sides as he barely kept himself from falling. She kept close, knowing that the power of that discipline lay in proximity. Knees and elbows. Constant attacks. She moved her legs in a flurry of hits, keeping him off balance. Her breath burned in her lungs as she fought with everything she had. She had to help her sisters.

Her legs were useless against Dorn, but her left arm

seemed strong enough to have at least some effect. She couldn't help wondering if it was just the strengthening effect of the wristbands or something else. That was her injured shoulder. She would think it would be the weaker side. Her shoulder and side were still stiff, but didn't hurt. That was a bonus.

Dorn spun away from her, and she used the opportunity to lash out and grab onto one of the pins in the fins running along his back. They were the only part of his body that looked potentially vulnerable. It worked even better than she'd hoped. His back arched and he dropped to one knee, gasping and clutching at the floor.

She was just about to knee him in the face when he let out a guttural groan that almost sounded like her name. The fin beneath her hand started to vibrate again, resonating up through the arm that held him and across her shoulders, lighting up her spine with pleasure that verged on ecstasy. The sensation sped down to her core and detonated with so much pleasure that she nearly climaxed from it.

She stumbled forward, catching herself with her other hand on his back. His muscles flexed beneath her palm, strong and firm. Her mind was flooded with a vision of his strong jaw and glowing green eyes. He was so gorgeous… And she could have him. Pull him to his feet, tear off their clothes, leap onto him and wrap her legs around his waist and let him drive himself deep into her. Hell, at this point, she'd almost be okay with him yanking her to the ground and pinning her beneath him.

Another wave of pleasure raged through her body, setting her nerves on fire and turning her belly molten. This was just from *touching* him. What would happen if she let him claim her? If this was what her sisters had experienced, maybe what they had gone through hadn't been bad at all.

No. No, this wasn't right. Amy had to resist. She and her sisters had been taken. Good guy aliens didn't abduct people. If her sisters had any choice in the matter, they would have been there when Amy woke up.

She shoved herself away from Dorn, staggering back as she tried to clear her head. From the corner of her eye, she could see Kral holding his hand over his mouth, his shoulders shaking as if he was laughing.

"What's so funny?" Amy said.

"You grabbed him by… a very sensitive part of our anatomy." Kral grinned.

Was that… It couldn't be his… Amy's cheeks burned even as her ardor chilled. That was not the kind of visual she had been imagining a moment before.

"Whatever kind of 'claiming' you think you have going on here, I don't think you're biologically compatible with Earthlings," she said. "I mean, if those are your…"

Dorn rose to his feet, his back to her and those damn fins still shimmering with the promise of more pleasure than she had ever known. She swallowed hard as he turned to face her, eyes glowing so brightly she could hardly hold his gaze.

"Those are my spine plates," Dorn said, his voice low and gravelly. He gestured toward the impressive bulge in the front of his pants. "These are my dicks, and I assure you, our species are extremely compatible."

She swallowed hard, her stare fixed on his…

Wait, did he say 'dicks?' As in plural?

His chest heaved and his hands flexed and relaxed, his fingertips much pointier then she remembered. He stared at her with his head lowered like a predator. A thrill shot through her that had nothing to do with their fighting.

"I'm here to witness a challenge, not a claiming," Kral said. "Either proceed or yield."

Amy wasn't about to yield. There was too much at stake. Too much that she didn't understand. She focused on the fight, pushing aside all other thoughts, as tantalizing as they were. Dorn had retreated to the other side of the room.

He wanted her. Everything about him screamed it, including the emotions he was projecting. In that moment, she believed them. She had to block it out, to stay rational as she examined her situation—no easy task when her body was doing its best to answer the call to him.

Taking deep breaths, she assessed what she had learned while they were sparring. It wasn't looking good for her at all. If she tried to reengage him, he would have a better opportunity to attack. The martial arts forms that used the attacker's momentum against them wouldn't be very effective given the way his mass was distributed—and there was a lot of it. She needed to get in close again to land attacks, but if he grabbed her, it would be over, and she wasn't even sure she would mind.

A thrill shot through her at the thought of *losing*. She wanted him to grab her, to hold her, to claim her. How could she feel that way? It didn't help that he kept feeding her positive emotions somehow. He was amused and fascinated by her, proud of her strength and skill. No one had ever expressed anything like that before. Not about her fighting skills.

Her family barely tolerated her dream of joining the FBI, acting like it was a childish indulgence that she would outgrow, even though she had dedicated her life to becoming the best agent she could once she was ready to join them. The only emotion they ever expressed regarding her 'hobbies' was concern.

Did Dorn know that? Was he purposefully choosing the emotions she most longed to have directed toward her?

"Your Earth fighting techniques are intriguing," he said, stalking back and forth in front of the wall of windows that gave a view of the speckled expanse of space behind him. "I look forward to learning more about them."

"I'd be happy to kick your ass again anytime."

He smiled, amusement and pride cascading through her, along with more of that damn lust. Warmth flooded her chest as the emotions she was sure he was purposefully projecting at her filled her. Dammit, she wouldn't fall for his tricks. But she was so out of her depth here. She was in *outer space*. What could she possibly use to her advantage?

There were no loose objects to use as weapons. Even the bed she'd been on was bolted to the floor. It made sense, with the threat of losing gravity or having a hull breach that could cause anything not strapped down to turn into a deadly weapon as it was sucked into the freezing void.

A dozen sci-fi movies that she had watched with her family popped into her mind, scenes with the vacuum of space pulling everything toward itself, and an idea began to take shape. An idea that made her stomach sour and her palms sweat. What she was considering was something she knew she might have to face in her career eventually. If she proceeded, then found out she was wrong about Dorn…

She shook herself internally. Her sisters' lives were on the line. Maybe Buddy's, as well, and even their parents. Amy didn't have the luxury of mercy.

Chapter Five

Something very frightening was rising up within his soulmate. A mixture of nerves and steely resolve. She was working herself up to something, and he had no idea what it was. He only knew that it would not be good for him, or perhaps for her as well. She paced the room, mirroring his movements as he did the same before the viewport behind him. Every pass widened, until they were nearly crossing the entire space. What would she do if he charged her?

The thought was beyond appealing. If he could just get close enough, he could grab her and hold her to his chest, crush her mouth with his, claim her as his mate in body, soul, and marriage. He wanted it so much, it was like a pressure building within him, pushing him to do… something. Something desperate.

His hearts pounded in his chest, the feeling rising within him. He didn't know if it was hers or his own. This had to stop before she was hurt. She had landed several incredible blows—strikes that should not have hit him as hard as they did. The wristbands would increase her strength, but not this much. The attacks from her left arm were much stronger than the right. Those tightened ligaments were definitely doing something extra.

"Amy, the healers need to look at your shoulder again," he said. "I think something is wrong."

"Looking for an excuse to bail?" She shook her head as she approached the medical bed in her prowling. "How disappointing."

"I'm not leaving your side," he said. "Never."

A wave of approval flowed out from her—one she quickly snuffed, but not before he sensed it. All that remained was a cold intention. She stepped to the foot of the bed, leaning against it. Was his plan working? The more proximity they shared, the more she must feel their bond. The less she could resist it. When she had grabbed his spine plates before, he had barely been able to keep himself from grabbing her and claiming her on the spot. The desire he sensed from her had driven him nearly mad with need. Soon, she would be his. Soon, she would give herself to him. He just had to get close enough to—

Amy raised her arms, quickly activating the blasters for both wristbands. The beams gouged blackened grooves along the floor of the room before reaching him, indicating they were at maximum power. He brought up his shields just in time, but the force of her attack pushed him backwards. Though his feet were braced, he slid to the viewport, his back slamming against it, flattening his spine plates.

Amy sank to the floor, keeping the blasts pressing against him. It was all he could do to keep the shield on his arm between them. Her wristbands didn't have limitless power, and the blasters required more than the shielding. He could wait until her energy gave out, but her icy determination of purpose was intensifying. She hooked her left knee around the bed's leg, positioning it behind her body. Why would she do that? Her lips pressed tightly together and her eyes blazed.

A new emotion rippled out from her. One that nearly froze the blood in his veins. Regret. She was about to do something she didn't truly wish to do. She was about to kill him. He didn't know how, but he was certain that was her intention.

"Amy," he ground out. "Stop. I yield. I yield!"

"That's not good enough," she said. "I can't trust you. Not when my family is at stake."

A loud *crick* sounded behind him. The transparent material of the viewport. She was trying to space him.

Kral dropped his arms from his chest and yelled, "Amy, stop. You win the challenge. Dorn has yielded."

"I don't care," she said.

Kral gestured toward the clear view of space behind Dorn. "You're going to break the viewport."

Through gritted teeth, she said, "That's the idea."

Her wristbands began to glow, the crystalline metal heating under the onslaught of too much raw power. Dorn could feel her pain, see it etched in the lines around her eyes and the way her lips were pulled back from her teeth, but she wasn't about to stop. He sent a desperate wave of warning to Kral through their own bond.

"Becca," Dorn barely managed. "Get Becca."

Kral nodded curtly, then vanished.

"Using my sister against me?" Amy said, her eyes glittering. "You're even worse than I thought."

"Amy, please. You don't understand."

She shook her head sharply. "I won't let you get in my head. You won't stop me."

She was right. The cracking sounds behind him were growing louder. Spreading. He was running out of time. Kral wouldn't be back before the viewport shattered. Amy might not be sucked out into space with how she'd anchored herself to the bed with her leg, but all the air in the room would, along with the heat. Radiation would flood the chamber. Her wristbands were at such a depleted power level, he wasn't sure how long her shields would last after she succeeded in blasting him into space. She could be hurt again. She might even die.

He couldn't let that happen. He would rather die himself. He would rather… That was it. It was the only way. For her to stop her attack, she had to think that she had won—on her terms.

This is going to hurt.

Dorn hummed a few notes, channeling more energy to

his whole-body shielding. He took a deep breath, focusing on quieting his thoughts, pulling his emotions deep within himself and stilling them. If this was going to work, he had to show no reaction, not even through their bond. She couldn't sense anything from him. He made his body jerk, then released his breath and slumped, dropping his arms to his sides.

Heat from the blast scorched his skin, penetrating through his personal shield. Pain arced through his nerves. He steeled himself against it, experiencing the pain as if it was outside of himself, using every ounce of mental control he possessed. Amy kept her blaster on him for several long seconds. He expected it—would have done the same in her place. Finally, the blast stopped. Dorn fell forward, not catching himself as he struck the hard floor. The impact barely registered, the remnants of the blaster's energy still lighting his nerves on fire. By the Maker, why did they make their wristbands so powerful?

He sensed her approach, the remorse flowing through her. Her sneakered feet padded lightly on the metal floor. If only she would come a bit closer, he could grab her and keep her from shooting him again. But she stayed out of his range, ever cautious.

"I'm sorry," she whispered, then turned and ran toward the other side of the room.

Amy had to escape while she could. Based on the layout of the room, she thought she had figured out where the door should be, but she had no idea how to open it. A large, rectangular panel stood before her, not opening at her approach. She glanced around it and didn't see any sort of access pad, knob, or button. There had to be a way out of this place. She couldn't be thwarted already. Not after what she had done.

The skin around her wristbands burned from the heat they'd put off in the fight. Overheating while she… While she…

Her vision blurred briefly. She had never killed anyone or anything before. Her chest felt hollowed out, an ache that went beyond anything she expected. She had only done what she had to. Her sisters needed her. Amy hadn't thought it would hit her so hard, given what was at stake. But, even with all her misgivings, there was something about Dorn she couldn't shake. Not that she believed his ludicrous story about them being soulmates.

There was no time to feel guilty. He had been preying on her by using some sort of alien abilities she didn't understand. She had to use this chance to escape while she could. She needed to locate a computer and see where her sisters were and find a way to get to them—if she could even figure out how to use it. What she had done was too terrible for her to fail now. Dorn was gone.

But, if he really was gone, why did she still feel as if he was with her, that odd energy resonating between them? The skin along her spine surged to life again, goosebumps racing up and down her back, arcing out along her shoulders and down her legs, so much stronger than before. Slowly, she turned to see Dorn rise to his feet.

A traitorous part of her was relieved beyond words, her heart light and racing and her breath coming easier. It wasn't just that she hadn't killed someone, but that she hadn't killed *him*. He was important to her, or he just wanted her to think so and was using some sort of alien power to make her believe it. She didn't know what to think.

The only thing she was sure of was that Dorn was not messing around anymore. The sparring before had been something like a game to him. She had felt his amusement several times, mixed with that heady pride. Now, there was purpose coursing out of him like a knife strike. She would get no second chances.

She could barely swallow, each pounding beat of her heart tightening her throat further. The trick with the viewport had only worked as well as it had because he wasn't expecting it. She had no advantages left. His green eyes glowed like twin nuclear reactors and a broad smile crossed his face as he once more watched her from beneath lowered brows, stalking toward her like she was prey.

A whooshing sound behind her caught her attention. She spun around to see two figures standing in the open door—one male, one female—both wearing the same silver catsuits with chrome helmets that the people who had attacked her and taken Sophie had been wearing. Dorn was working with them after all.

Panic welled up in Amy, a sharp, stabbing memory of pain throbbing through her shoulder. Her mouth went dry and the chamber felt like it was spinning around her. She had almost fallen for it. This was a trap. All of it. Her eyes blurred as the pain spread to her heart. How could Dorn's betrayal hurt so much when they had only just met? There was no way it was because of all that soulmate bullshit.

She lifted her arm and slammed her hand on the white button on her wristband, ignoring how it made the burns around them sear while she blasted the woman on her right. A brief flash of blue flickered over her as she sailed back into the hallway beyond. Before the man could respond, Amy lashed out with her left elbow, catching him on the side of his helmet. As he staggered to the side, she caught him in the ribs with a bone-crunching kick. Whatever this pair was underneath the suits, they weren't as tough as Dorn. The man went down on one knee as Amy ran past.

The hallway was at least fifteen feet high and broad enough for five men to walk shoulder-to-shoulder. The floors were gunmetal gray, with gleaming white walls curving up from them to form an arching ceiling. Amy glanced both ways, not seeing a difference one way or another. She needed time, a distraction, anything to give her a chance to get away. Spinning back around, she ran her fingertip along the white button for her wristbands' blaster until it was as bright as it could be, then slammed her hand on it, her arm pointed at the weakened section of viewport.

The blast hurtled past Dorn, crashing into the exposed glass. Cracks spread out from the impact point, but Amy couldn't stick around to finish the job. She had to trust that she'd done enough damage to distract him, if not suck him into space. She barely had time to register the way his eyes widened and his mouth dropped open in horror as he turned toward the expanding crack in the station's exterior before her eyes filled with tears again. Blinking them away, she turned to sprint down the hallway, but someone grabbed her ankle, tripping her. Amy fell forward, her chin hitting the floor hard. The coppery taste of blood filled her mouth.

Flipping onto her back, she lashed out with her free foot, hitting the woman on the side of the helmet. The force of the blow knocked the woman's head against the wall and her hand loosened enough for Amy to free herself. She did a backwards roll over her shoulders, coming up in a crouch. The hallway was spinning pretty good after the blow she'd taken hitting the floor, but she knew she couldn't stay here.

Amy ran down the hall just as Dorn emerged from the chamber, carrying the man in the silver suit that she had fought. She glanced back in time to see the door whoosh shut behind him. A red light flashed angrily above it and a loud siren began to blare, hurting her ears. The woman was on her feet already, her arm rising to point at Amy with one of those goddammed bracers.

Dorn smacked the woman's arm down and yelled, "Don't engage!" moving to stand between her and Amy.

Her heart swelled with warmth. He was protecting her. She shook herself. No, he was working with the people who had hurt her. The people who had taken Sophie. He'd admitted that his people were holding Amy's sisters. She didn't know what his goal was this time, but if he thought she'd be fooled again, he was mistaken. She turned and ran as fast as she could around a bend in the hallway, desperately searching for a place to hide and regroup, to get her head straight and, more importantly, her heart.

Chapter Six

Dorn kept himself between the Coalition soldiers assigned to guard *Outreach* station and Amy's retreating form. She didn't look back as she turned a curve in the corridor, disappearing from view. Goddess, she was fierce! The soldier he had rescued tapped on the side of his helmet. Lines appeared in the smooth chrome surface as the panels of the helmet tilted, then swept back over his head to fold into the collar around his uniform's neck. Dorn recognized him as Rin, the medic who had been assigned to assist with Amy's healing.

Irony.

Rin gasped for breath, one arm holding his ribs. "Holy fuck, did she just try to space us?"

Dorn did his best not to smile, but failed. "No. She tried to kill us."

"That…" Rin shook his head. "That does not make me feel better. I think she broke some ribs."

"Let's get you to the next medical bay," Dorn said. He nodded to the woman, who was on her feet, but wobbly. "You, too. And while we walk, let your command know that they are not to approach Amy under any circumstances. Let her cool down while we assess the damage done to both you and the station." He glared at one of the red lights above, the piercing klaxon of their alarm making his ears ring. "And turn off that damned noise."

The woman nodded, reaching out to balance herself with the wall as they walked the short distance to the next medical bay. The door opened for them, and he waited for her to catch up, hoping she wasn't too addled to follow his commands properly. Once they were inside, she retracted her helmet, revealing short brown hair and large green eyes set in an overly angular face. Typical Sadirian.

"That was incredible," she said. "Your blasters are so much more powerful than ours. I don't understand why I wasn't vaporized."

"I shielded you," Dorn said. "Otherwise, you would have been."

She shook her head. "Are you sure it's safe to let that Earthling have the run of the station?"

Dorn helped Rin sit on the edge of a regen bed, then turned back to the female soldier. "What's your name?"

"T-61-d5." She stood straighter, arms clamped to her sides and only a trace of her earlier dizziness evident by the slight weaving in her stance.

Dorn's hearts gave a tug as he shook his head. "I asked for your name, not the label the genetic engineers gave you."

"Oh." Her eyes widened a bit and her cheeks pinked. "Taig, sir."

Dorn did his best to keep his voice gentle. "This station was built with Coalition, Antarean, and Vegan technology, correct?"

"Yes, sir," Taig said.

"Then I imagine you can track a single Earthling using your scanners." He suppressed the urge to laugh at the chagrined expression that swept her features. "Don't worry about it. My shields couldn't completely protect you, so you're bound to not be thinking too clearly yet. Relay that information to your superiors while I get Rin settled in the regen bed, then find your own to heal any damage you sustained."

"Yes, sir."

"Hey, I'm the medic here," Rin said, his eyes pinched with pain. "I should examine you both."

He started to rise, but Dorn pushed him firmly onto the bed. "I'm fine. And all Taig has to do is lie down in one of the chambers and the regen bed will take care of the rest. They're one of the few things the Coalition got right. Well, aside from using them to mentally program your soldiers."

"We don't do that anymore," Rin said. "Besides, the Vegans oversaw every step of this station's construction. They wouldn't have let anything like that slip past them."

Dorn had his doubts about that. The station was huge,

and there was no way the Vegans could oversee every aspect of its construction. With some Sadirians still operating with subconscious mental programming left over from the High Council, Dorn knew there was always a chance for surprises. He kept his thoughts to himself, wanting only to get these soldiers the help they needed so that he could go find his soulmate—his wife.

A smile quirked his lips at the thought. Amy had challenged him and won. His chest swelled with pride at her skill and ingenuity, his hearts racing both with excitement at being bonded and the adrenaline surge he could still sense from her through their connection. She had found a place where she felt relatively safe and was calming herself, focusing her thoughts. He could use this time to check in with Kral and let him know what had happened.

As if summoned, the holoprojector in the room flickered on, creating an image of not only Kral, but Becca as well. Her dark hair was pulled back in a long ponytail and she wore the standard Earth fare that Dorn had always seen her in—a pale T-shirt, jeans, and sturdy boots. Her dark eyes, so like Amy's, flashed with anger and concern as she glanced around the room.

"Where is Amy?" Becca demanded.

"Safe." Dorn turned back to Rin and helped the medic lie down in the regen bed. Once his legs were within the chamber, Dorn stepped back and activated the unit. The clear, cylindrical dome arched over him, sealing the bed. Lights flooded the chamber, beams scanning him and beginning repairs. Rin's eyes fluttered shut, and the tightness of his features smoothed, the regen bed placing him in stasis as it did its work.

Dorn turned to Taig and said, "Now you."

She nodded curtly. "Yes, sir. And I've passed your recommendations on to command. They'll comply with your wishes, but only to a point. That Earthling did a lot of damage to the medical bay. The viewport blew out right after you two exited the room."

Of course it did. Dorn had been projecting a shield over it while they made their escape. He didn't bother telling Taig. She already knew more about his Cygnian wristbands' capabilities than Dorn liked. The power drain had been significant, but the station's lighting would recharge his wristbands in an hour or so. They would also be recharging Amy's, making her more dangerous. He smiled, wondering about what surprises their next encounter would hold.

"Into the bed with you," Dorn said, gesturing to the nearest open regen bed.

Taig arched an eyebrow, but hopped up onto the white cushioned interior. She laughed as she stretched out in it, folding her hands over her stomach.

"What?" Dorn asked.

"I thought you were the Cygnians' security guy," she

said. "But you have the bedside manner of a medic."

A thread of pain lanced through him, his hearts beating faster as memories threatened to surface that he didn't have time to deal with now. Not many Cygnians acted as nursemaid for another. Dorn wished to the Maker that he had never had the chance.

"The station needs every soldier at the ready," Dorn said. He leaned in and added, "Especially with my wife on the loose."

Taig's eyes widened, and her head lifted from the small pillow beneath it. Before she could say anything, Dorn pressed the button to seal her in and stepped back, smirking. He wanted everyone to know that Amy was his. First, he should probably explain that to Amy, though. When he turned, his smile faded under Becca's harsh glare.

"Wife?" she ground out.

"Um…" Kral gestured toward Dorn and said, "Amy challenged him."

"There is no way she would have done that if she knew she was challenging him for his hand in marriage," Becca said.

"Amy has all of me." Dorn looked from one hand to the other before dropping his arms back to his sides. "Why would Earthlings be interested in marrying a single body part?"

"It's an expression," Becca said through gritted teeth.

"Amy wouldn't have challenged you if she had thought it might end up with you being married."

"Why didn't you just say that?" Dorn shook his head. "Earth expressions are baffling."

"Challenging someone to combat to marry them is baffling," Becca snapped.

"We are still learning each other's ways," Kral said "But according to our tradition and our law, Amy and Dorn are married. She challenged him."

"And won," Dorn said, his chest puffing out with pride.

Becca's brow furrowed, a deep frown pulling at her lips as she glared at Dorn. "My baby sister defeated you in a challenge?"

"It would seem she has skills that you kept from us," Dorn said.

"None that would enable her to beat you in a fair fight." Becca crossed her arms over her chest, the challenge blazing in her eyes *almost* concealing the brief moment of doubt that flickered across her features.

"Take care, Becca," Dorn said. "You will be our queen someday and have shown respect for our ways up to now. The challenge is one of the most sacred aspects of our culture. No Cygnian would dare taint it by not bringing their full potential to it. The challenge is how we prove ourselves worthy as mates. I admit that I didn't take the threat Amy presented as seriously as I should have at first, but I assure you, she defeated me soundly through her cunning and strength."

"Dammit." Becca let out a breath, her arms dropping to her sides.

"Is it such a bad thing?" Kral asked. "We've discussed how we might modify the challenge so that you and I and the other soulmate pairs could be properly bonded—married."

"Yeah, by letting us choose the time, venue, and mode of the challenge," Becca said. "None of which Amy did. How the hell did she beat him?" She gestured toward Dorn and let out an exasperated sigh.

"You underestimate her," Dorn said. "Watch the recording."

"What recording?" Becca asked.

"All challenges are recorded for the archives," Kral said. "As well as being witnessed by those close to the pair. I observed Amy during the majority of the battle, and she was magnificent."

"And you left before we were joined by two Coalition soldiers," Dorn gestured to the regen beds. "Both of whom are now in regen beds after their encounter with Amy."

"You're kidding." Becca's eyes widened in surprise. More of that doubt crossed her expression, but this time, it remained. "I always thought it was a phase. Just a game she was playing."

Dorn took a step closer. "What game?"

Becca hesitated for several moments, then said, "Since

she was a kid, Amy's always had this thing about becoming like a superhero."

"A superhero?" Dorn asked, eager to learn more about his mate.

"Yeah, like a human with superpowers—or at least super-training," Becca said. "We tried to talk her out of it, but she wouldn't listen, so we just kind of ignored it."

"Why would you discourage her?" Dorn asked.

"Because she's our baby sister," Becca snapped. "And the things she's been learning about are dangerous."

Dorn and Kral exchanged a glance as Becca continued to scowl, her focus locked on nothing in particular. Kral was the one brave enough to prod her from her thoughts.

"Such as?" he prompted.

"Like martial arts and weapons," Becca said. "I can't even pronounce the names of half the types of black belts she's earned, and she'd study with these really seedy types sometimes. Street fighting." Becca rolled her eyes. "She spent tons of time at the range, learning about different firearms and becoming a crack shot. She even studied things like archery and whatever weapons her martial arts teachers would train her on."

"Earth has not achieved world peace yet," Kral said. "Did she expect to be part of a conflict?"

"No." Becca shook her head. "Well, not exactly. She wants to join the FBI."

"The what?" Kral asked.

"The Federal Bureau of Investigation." Becca shook her head. "It's like a really high-level law enforcement agency."

"So, it's a group that handles security," Dorn clarified.

"I guess," Becca shrugged.

Security. His mate had trained for most of her life to join an agency responsible for the security of others. An elite agency, from the sound of it. Dorn's hearts filled with pride once more, their strong, near-unified beat reminding him of the closeness of his soulmate. He couldn't wait to claim her fully, to join in unity and feel their souls merge into one. He tried to mask his smile, but it wouldn't be confined. From the way Kral's shoulders shook, he was in much the same situation. Finally, both men threw their heads back and laughed, while Becca regarded them as if they'd gone mad.

"My mate is not fierce," Dorn said, "she is *ferocious*."

"And shares your skill in tactical awareness and combat ability." Kral shook his head, still smiling. "Brother, I am so happy for you. I formally recognize your bond and will send the recording of your challenge to the archives."

Becca opened her mouth, brow furrowed as if she was about to protest, but then she snapped her jaw shut and shook her head. "All those classes she took. You should know, it isn't just fighting she learned about. She also studied how to use her environment to her advantage.

Infiltration, technology even. She's better with computers than any of us."

"She certainly used her environment to defeat you," Kral said.

Dorn nodded, but his smile became subdued. "Infiltration. Does that mean she's good at hiding?"

"I guess that's part of it," Becca said. "She can be so freaking annoying. There was no way to hide anything from her, and she always seemed to know whatever was going on. I thought it was just because she was the annoying little sibling, you know?"

Dorn didn't know. He had never felt anything but love, guilt, and mind-numbing fear where his younger sibling was concerned. Now, they did their best to ignore the bond of their blood in their interactions. If they weren't in the same prism, they would probably never speak. As it was, Dorn doubted the others even knew that they were brothers by birth as well as by the soul bond shared among the warriors.

An alert sounded in the room before the comm became active. Dorn didn't recognize the voice, but from the sibilance in it, he would bet it was a Vegan.

"Pardon the intrusion, but we wanted to let you know that Amy has disappeared from our scans," he said.

Becca's eyes widened and her mouth dropped open again. Dorn only laughed. Amy might be able to hide from the station's systems, but she couldn't hide from their soulmate bond. Still, he needed to find her before she got into more trouble. He had given her all the time he could. Turning, Dorn strode to the door.

"I'll find her," he called over his shoulder.

"Buddy is on the *Reckoning*," Kral said. "We'll contact him and have him join you to help Amy… adjust."

"Dorn." There was an edge of desperation in Becca's tone that made Dorn pause. "She's still my baby sister. Go easy on her when you find her."

"It's past time you accepted that Amy is not a child." Dorn smirked as he headed for the door. "And who will be there to tell her to go easy on me?"

Chapter Seven

The corridor seemed to go on forever, an endless expanse of plain white walls and gunmetal gray floor passing by Amy as she ran. If it weren't for the occasional branching hallway, she would have felt as though she was running in place, the station moving around her. Her lungs burned and her heart pounded in her chest so hard, she thought it might burst. She kept herself in top shape, but the stress was starting to catch up with her. She needed to find a place to regroup and think.

Amy had passed several rooms as she ran, but didn't dare enter them. It would be all too easy for someone to pin her down again if she did. Wherever she went, she couldn't let herself be trapped. The window she had blasted had a slight curve to it, the same as the hallway she was in. Hopefully, that meant she was sticking to the edge of the station. Going deeper down one of the connecting hallways didn't seem wise, but if she could find a place where their ships docked, she might be able to commandeer one and use it to get to her sisters in the asteroid belt. She'd gladly coerce one of the silver-suited goons into taking her there.

How was this her life? It didn't seem possible that she was running from aliens and trying to find a spaceship to steal. The only part of this whole experience that felt real was that seven foot blue alien. Not the soulmates part—that was for fairy tales. She could never let herself believe in something so outlandish and… magical. No, she had to be pragmatic. Dorn had tricked her. He was working with the same people who had kidnapped her sisters and almost killed her.

Amy's eyes burned as she fought back tears. She had almost started believing him that there was some sort of connection between them. She *wanted* to believe him. Who wouldn't? But it was all a lie. She pushed her thoughts of him as far out of her mind as she could—which she realized wasn't nearly far enough.

An archway stood open in the corridor ahead. She slowed as she approached. It was the first branch in the corridor she had encountered that went off to her right. If she had any chance of staying on the outskirts of the station, she probably needed to take that path.

No one had approached her, which only raised her suspicions. Were they herding her into a trap? She couldn't imagine a station as advanced as this one not having the ability to track her. Not only did she have to find a place to hide, it had to be off their grid.

Great.

Mouth dry from nerves and exertion, she plastered herself to the wall next to the open archway, then peered around the corner. The room inside was huge and filled with metallic crates, barrels, and boxes. Was it a cargo hold? Whatever it was, it was a perfect hiding place. There was plenty of cover and she'd be able to weave in and out among the spaces between the cargo if necessary.

She crept into the room, sticking close to the wall until she could dart across to an opening between two tall stacks of metal crates. Noting each turn and counting her steps, she created a mental map of the area. Deep in the storage space, she found a small alcove formed from a grouping of different sized boxes. It was just big enough for her to crawl inside. She'd still be able to hear people approach, but wouldn't feel as exposed. All she needed was a few minutes to collect herself and quiet her breathing and heart rate. She tucked herself into the small space and wrapped her arms around her knees, hugging them against her heaving chest.

Deep breaths. In… Out… Clear my mind. Look at things rationally.

Her breathing steadied and her heart calmed, but the tightness in her chest remained. Was it a panic attack? It didn't seem to match the symptoms she'd read about. She didn't feel like she was about to die or even that something awful was about to happen to her. Something awful might happen to the people who *found* her, though.

Part of her still couldn't believe that she had tried to kill someone. Several someones, including the big, blue alien. She hated to admit it, but she was glad he was okay.

What was wrong with her? These aliens had abducted her sisters and were holding them against their will. Okay, they were holding Becca against her will. If all of the blue guys were as hot as Kral and Dorn, Sophie would be throwing herself at them. And if they could do that pheromone whammy to anyone… Amy shuddered, traces of the pleasure Dorn had evoked in her weaving through her body.

Why were they being targeted? And how did Buddy figure into all of this? Her brother had said he'd been hanging out with Kral for a while. The two seemed to have a rapport at the family dinner Kral had crashed. Buddy had been eager to get Kral to leave, though. There had been that weird chemistry between Becca and Kral as well.

Maybe Buddy knew about the pheromones and was trying to keep the blue guys away from his sisters. Amy could totally believe that, but it didn't explain why the blue guys were working with the people who had broken into their house and shot her. Amy was missing something. Some piece to the puzzle that would make it all fit together.

"Human." A firm, yet tiny feminine voice beside her made Amy jump.

How did they sneak up on her? She glanced out at the

path between the crates, but didn't see anyone.

"What are you doing?" the voice said, a distinctly childlike quality to it.

Amy looked down to see a small calico kitten staring at her with large golden eyes. Her fluffy fur was white and looked as soft as a cloud, with little splashes of cream, cinnamon, and mocha on her ears and along her back. A silver collar gleamed around her neck. Amy's heart seemed to pause, then it started thudding in her chest again.

In a family full of dog people, all Amy had ever wanted was a cat. This was the most gorgeous, adorable kitten she'd ever seen. The kitten stepped forward, opening her mouth to let out a long meow.

"What are you doing?"

Amy shook her head. She would have sworn the childlike voice was coming from the kitten, but that would be absolutely crazy.

"Human!" The kitten hissed, stalking closer. The voice really did seem to be coming from her, overlapping her meows. "I asked you a question. I expect an answer."

Amy let out a little laugh. She shook her head and looked away, pinching her eyes shut.

Silver spacesuits, blue aliens, ray guns and blasters. All of that, Amy could somehow handle. But an utterly adorable kitten who could talk was just too much. Something that amazing and wonderful couldn't be plopped down in the middle of all this terribleness. The walls of carefully controlled thought and logic Amy had erected around her mind broke down, errant dreams crashing through them.

She *wanted* soulmates to be real. Who in their right mind wouldn't want to find someone who could fulfill them in ways no one else could? Someone who would understand them and support them and protect them, exploring all life had to offer side-by-side for the rest of their existence? And if Dorn was her soulmate, how much of a bonus would that be? He was the most gorgeous man she'd ever seen. If he had approached her without all the drama, she'd have wanted to see where things went between them.

But there *was* drama. And kidnapping. And blasters and pain.

"Human," the kitten said again. "What—are—you—do—ing—here?"

Between every syllable, Amy felt a teeny paw whack her arm. The sentence ended with a prolonged hiss that had Amy giggling.

"Are you… Are you *laughing* at me?" The kitten's eyes were wide when Amy looked at her again, her voice filled with disbelief. She was sitting back on her haunches, both paws raised as if she was going to start batting at Amy again, only this time her claws were extended.

Amy pinched her lips together, fighting back more

laughter. She shook her head, and said, "No. Never."

The kitten slowly lowered her paws to the floor. Her eyes narrowed and her ears flattened against her head. "I think you *are* laughing at me. And you will regret it."

"I didn't mean to offend you," Amy hurried to say. Now that the dam was open, she couldn't stop the words from gushing forth. "Honestly, I didn't. Meeting you is the best thing that's happened to me since… ever. You are amazing and I'm in awe of you and I can't believe I'm talking to a kitten."

The kitten cocked her head to the side, her ears slowly rising. She looked off to the side and sniffed. "I suppose I can take you at your word then."

"My name is Amy." She couldn't believe she was having a conversation with a cat. An intelligent cat! She'd had dreams like this when she was younger, before she'd decided to focus all of her mental energy on her training.

"I'm Queenie."

Another laugh bubbled up in Amy's chest. She barely stopped it in time, coughing to disguise what sound escaped.

"I didn't mean not to answer you before," Amy said. "I'm kind of overwhelmed right now, so I came here to hide."

Queenie snorted. "The station has scanners, you know."

"I figured." Amy sighed, her shoulders slumping.

Queenie took a few steps closer and lowered her voice.

"But there is a place the scanners don't reach. I can show you."

A place with no scanners? Amy could really be safe there. Safer, anyway. She could brainstorm and maybe ask Queenie some questions. The little kitten seemed like an unlikely ally. An incredibly unlikely, absolutely adorable ally.

'Adorable' didn't seem like a word Queenie would like. Amy made a mental note to avoid using it.

"I would really appreciate that," Amy said.

"Well, come on then." Queenie turned and scampered down the path between the crates.

Amy scrambled out of her cramped hiding place, following as Queenie jumped up onto a box, then another and another till she was on top of the stack. Amy had to climb more than hop, but was grateful the kitten was small and couldn't make leaps across spaces bigger than Amy could manage. They navigated the tops of the cargo, jumping across the narrow spaces between stacks until they reached the edge of the main group of crates. Amy's stomach was full of butterflies and her head spun a little.

"I don't feel right," Amy said.

"That's the gravity." Queenie crouched down before a gap that was much wider than any they'd crossed yet. The crates across from them were higher as well. "It's not as strong here. The station's systems don't quite reach this spot—including the scanners."

“What about life support?”

Queenie made a little scoffing noise, then leapt from the crate. Amy gasped, her heart seizing in her chest as she realized how far up they had climbed. She reached out to catch the kitten, but stopped as she saw her float across the space. Queenie landed on the box on the other side of the gap, claws scraping the metal as she turned in that odd slow-motion Amy had seen in videos of the lunar landing or on feeds from Earth’s ‘human-built’ space station.

“Here goes nothing,” Amy said. She coiled herself, visualizing how she wanted her jump to go, then she made the leap.

Chapter Eight

It didn't take long for Amy's stomach to settle down and her equilibrium to return once she had settled onto the crates at the far end of the cargo hold. They must be at least forty feet from the ground. The outer hull of the station was right behind them, which was a mixed blessing. No one could sneak up behind them, but she had less room to maneuver if she was engaged. Queenie had explained where the low gravity area extended, and warned that if you fell off the crate or didn't make the jump across on the way back, gravity would reassert itself a few feet down and you'd be in for a very rough landing.

Amy flattened herself on the crate, peering down over the cargo hold. From their vantage point, they could see the main door plus another, bigger exit across from them. Based on the size of the opening, she would bet that's where they brought in the larger cargo items—and that there were ships beyond. She was close, but she needed a plan. One wrong move could get her captured again, and then where would her sisters be?

"You look like you're ready to pounce on someone."

Queenie's eyes widened, her voice lowering. "Are we pouncing on someone?"

The kitten stretched out on the crate, making her body as flat as possible. Even her ears lowered, sticking out to the sides adorably. Her whiskers perked up and she wiggled her back feet and hips, then let out a low meow.

"I want to pounce on someone," Queenie whispered, her pupils dilating till the gold of her irises was just a narrow ring.

Amy's heart filled with warmth. She already loved this little girl.

"We aren't pouncing," Amy said. "We're hiding."

"Oh."

How could a kitten make one word sound so full of judgmental disappointment?

"How boring." Queenie sat up, her tail flicking in irritation. "Who are we hiding from?"

"Everyone."

Queenie cocked her head to the side and turned to regard Amy, her interest once again piqued. "Are you a bad guy then?"

"What? No." Amy shook her head. Did Queenie not know the kind of people she was living with? "I'm the good guy."

Queenie scoffed, one ear angled back as she looked at the hold once more. "That's always a matter of perspective."

"I disagree." Amy rolled to her side and said, "Three of these silver-suited goons broke into my house and tried to kill my sister. They nearly killed me instead and they took my sisters after. Does that sound like something 'good guys' would do?"

Queenie was silent for a moment, then she let out a soft chirruping meow. The overlapping words were equally subdued. "I guess not." After a few more moments, she said, "What's your plan?"

"They were stupid enough to give me these wristbands and explain how they work. I don't think they realized I could actually use them. So I'm going to find a pilot and force him to take me to Ceres so I can rescue my sisters."

"That doesn't sound like something a good guy does."

Amy scowled. "That big blue guy is using some kind of alien pheromones to try to manipulate me." Her fingers clenched into fists, nails stinging as they dug into her palms. "I think some of his friends have already used them on my sisters. If they did, I'm going to track them down and kill them during my rescue operation."

"Still not sounding very much like a good guy," Queenie murmured. She glanced back at Amy and said, "Wait, 'big blue guy'… Are you talking about a Cygnian?"

"That's what he called himself. His name is Dorn." A shiver traveled up Amy's spine just from saying his name, her skin rising in goosebumps.

That son of a bitch.

"This doesn't make sense," Queenie said. "Cygnians are honorable warriors. They revere all females. Their planet doesn't have many left, so they appreciate us more than most species."

"Oh great," Amy clenched her jaw tight enough that her teeth ached. "They're looking for breeders."

Queenie crinkled up her nose. "Ew, gross. And *wrong*. They're looking for soulmates."

Amy snorted and rolled her eyes. "Not you, too."

"What?"

"There's no such thing as soulmates."

Amy swore the kitten smirked at her. One side of her cute little face arched up, and her whiskers were twitching as if she was stifling a laugh.

"Excuse me," Queenie said, "but I would be willing to bet a week's worth of treats that before today, you would have said the same thing about this space station or giant blue aliens."

Amy scoffed and shook her head.

"Or talking kittens?" Queenie prodded, her tone teasing.

Amy had to give her that. Her lips quirked up in a smile despite her situation.

"Okay, you have me there," Amy said. "But I'm not ready to believe that these are the good guys. They shot me. If I hadn't jumped in front of Sophie, they would have shot her. And they took her and Becca."

"Wait, Becca and Sophie..." Queenie turned to her, gold eyes wide and a tremor entering her voice. "Buddy Myers's sisters?"

How the heck did this kitten know about Buddy? And why did it make her so nervous to find out who her sisters were to him?

"Yes," Amy said. "I'm his sister, too."

"Oh." Queenie swallowed hard. She looked back at the cargo hold, her tail twitching fitfully behind her.

"Why does that freak you out?"

"I'm not freaked out," Queenie snapped, a definite hiss beneath her tone. "You're freaked out."

"Yeah, I am. Especially now that I'm afraid my only friend on this station is holding something back from me."

Queenie turned her big eyes at Amy, and said, "We're friends?"

"I wouldn't follow just anyone up here," Amy said. "I'm trusting you to help me. And I'll do what I can to help you, too."

Queenie made a series of chittering sounds. Amy had heard cats make a similar noise while watching birds in the videos she watched whenever she needed a break from her studies or just life in general. Whatever they meant to a cat, no understandable words accompanied the sound.

"I *will* help you." Queenie reached out and placed her paw on Amy's hand. "But the first thing we need to do is figure out who your enemies truly are."

"Dorn is at the top of that list," Amy said.

Queenie shook her head. "I don't think so. Have you been feeling a kind of zinging along your back? And prickly skin, like when someone pets you the wrong way and your fur stands on end?"

That was an odd way to put it, but then again, for a kitten it made sense. Amy nodded, a heavy feeling growing in her stomach, even in the lower gravity.

"That isn't pheromones," Queenie said. "It's the soulmate bond."

"I don't believe in soulmates."

Queenie angled her head again. "Just because you don't believe something, that doesn't mean it isn't true."

Damn, this kitten made some good points.

"Fine, let's say he is my soulmate," Amy said. "Why is he working with people who tried to kill me? Why are they holding my sisters?"

"They aren't. My family and I only moved to the station a few days ago. Before that, we lived on the *Reckoning*. It's a ship that's protecting the Sol system." Queenie's voice grew more animated as she talked. She stood and paced next to Amy, her long fur extra-fluffy from the low gravity. "My mom's sentient is Marq, the Commander of the *Reckoning*. He doesn't always realize we're in the room or listening when he has meetings. Becca and Kral came on board along with all the Cygnian warriors. They wanted our help to find Sophie. After

Sophie was rescued, Marq was talking to his wife about how lucky we are that Becca is Kral's soulmate."

"Becca… and Kral…" Amy's brain shied away from imagining Becca in a long term relationship with anyone. Her sister's standards were beyond high, and she put family above everything. Amy hadn't met a single guy Becca had dated. None of them were important enough to be introduced to the family.

Tumblers fell into place in Amy's mind as she remembered how Kral had shown up unexpectedly at their family dinner. He had said and done strange things that Amy had written off as just social awkwardness. Now, she knew that he was an alien who probably didn't know that much about their culture. But the thing she fixated on was the odd energy between Becca and Kral. The pair had moments when they seemed almost mesmerized by each other. Becca's cheeks had been rosy the whole time, her pupils dilated. She had been more worked up by Kral than Amy had ever seen her sister before. Was it because they actually were… soulmates?

What was it Dorn had said? That he carried the other half of Amy's soul?

A shiver passed through her at the thought. To be that intimately connected to anyone was utterly terrifying—and exhilarating at the same time. What did that mean about their autonomy? What if she didn't want to be with Dorn or they weren't a match in personality or values?

Amy pushed those thoughts aside, trying to focus on this new piece of the puzzle and how it applied to her current situation.

"Why would Marq think it's a good thing that Becca and Kral are soulmates?" Amy asked.

"Because he's the Crown Prince of Cygnus-Prime," Queenie said.

Amy's mind spun. "Does that mean one day my sister will be their queen?"

Queenie sat back down and tilted her head briefly to the side in an approximation of a shrug. "If the current queen, his mother, Ehmach, recognizes the pairing, I suppose so. I heard Marq talking with the Station Commander about it and apparently Kral told him that his mom isn't happy that their soulmates are Earthlings. That's why my mother and brother and sister and I had to move to the station—at least, when they aren't with their other sentients. Marq is worried that Ehmach might come to the Sol system and start a fight and didn't want us on the *Reckoning* if that happens."

Okay, Amy was starting to like this Marq guy. Anyone who was worried about kittens scored points in her book.

"I don't suppose Marq is a Cygnian as well," Amy said.

"No, he's Sadirian. He looks just like an Earthling." Queenie made the chittering noise again and lowered her head, then said, "You should know, he's part of the Coalition."

“I haven’t heard that term yet,” Amy said.

“They’re the ones who wear the silver spacesuits.” Before Amy could even form a thought, Queenie leapt forward. “But he’s not a bad guy. His crew aren’t bad guys, either.”

Queenie’s momentum was stronger than she realized. She scrabbled at the crate as she drifted toward Amy, but couldn’t find anything to grip with her claws. Amy reached out and grabbed her, pulling the kitten against her side. As soon as she did, Queenie started up again. It was hard for Amy to mind, with the soft, warm kitten snuggling up to her.

“The Coalition used to be the bad guys, but now they’re the good guys and most of them are trying to do the right thing,” Queenie said. “There are still some that miss how things used to be, which was really, really bad, though. I can’t believe that Marq or any of the Cygnians were involved in the attack on you and your sisters.”

“Okay, okay,” Amy said. “Just give me a minute to think.”

The information Queenie was giving her made sense, but Amy wasn’t sure she could trust it. Everything the kitten was telling Amy was what she wanted to hear. Could she even trust *herself* anymore? Where Dorn was involved, Amy wasn’t sure. There definitely had been something between them. The question remained, was he trying to manipulate her emotions on purpose, or was it just a side effect of—

She pinched her eyes shut and shook her head. This was all fantasy. She wasn't even sure she believed in souls, let alone that hers was tied to a gorgeous blue warrior. She and Dorn might be linked somehow, but even if they were, that meant their free will had been removed from the equation. She was so not okay with that. Whoever she ended up with, she wanted them to want her for who she was, not because of some mystical connection. Whether it was real or not, she wasn't interested. Her heart clenched at the thought, the skin on the inside of her arms tingling as if they could feel the absence of someone they were supposed to hold.

This wasn't good. Amy needed to get a handle on this before things went any further.

"You have to know that if Dorn wanted to force you into anything, he could easily do so," Queenie said. "He's a trained warrior, nearly indestructible, and incredibly strong. All Cygnians are."

"Yeah? Well I just kicked his a— butt," Amy quickly corrected. Queenie was a child, after all. Just to be sure her fix stuck, Amy repeated, "His butt."

"You?" Queenie twisted her head to look over at Amy. "Kicked a Cygnian warrior's butt?"

"I did."

Queenie snickered.

"I'm serious. I maneuvered him against a window and

held him there with my blaster. If the jerk face hadn't pretended to die, I would have kept it up till the glass broke and he was sucked into space."

"He pretended to die?" Queenie said, one eye pinched and her lips curling up in a long meow.

"We call it playing possum where I'm from. When I wouldn't accept that he yielded, he pretended he was dead so I would stop trying to kill him."

Queenie laughed, then shook her head. "Wait a minute." She turned back to Amy and stood, her eyes wide. "He yielded to you. He didn't challenge you to battle, did he?"

"No." Amy snorted. "He would have loved that, but I didn't give him the chance. I challenged him."

"Human, be very clear about this." Queenie stood and put one of her paws on Amy's arm. "You challenged your Cygnian soulmate to battle, and while you were fighting, he yielded."

"Yeah." Why was the little kitten being so dramatic? The way her eyes widened made Amy's stomach clench. She had a very bad feeling about this.

"That's… That's…" Queenie's eyes pinched shut and she let out a yowl overlaid with laughter. She fell onto her back, paws holding her stomach as she kept laughing. When she could gather enough breath, she gasped out, "That is the funniest thing I've ever heard."

Amy rolled onto her side, pride stinging. "I'm no

pushover. I've trained to fight my whole life."

Queenie paused, blinked a few times, then said, "That just makes it better," and went right back to laughing.

Amy scowled, waiting for the kitten to get it out of her system. It was hard to stay mad at Queenie when she was so damned cute. Finally, the little calico seemed to have finished. She rolled to her side, purring loudly. Amy's heart filled with warmth at the sound and the sight of the little fluffball staring at her with those big golden eyes. She couldn't resist reaching out and petting Queenie's tummy, holding her breath to see how the kitten would react. Her purring grew louder and her eyes half-closed.

"Now that you're done, mind telling me what's so funny?" Amy asked.

A huge grin stretched Queenie's face, her whiskers twitching. The kitten rose to her feet, then placed her paw back on Amy's hand.

"Cygnians are a warrior people," Queenie said.

"Yeah. So?" Amy was missing something. She wished Queenie would just come out and say it.

Until she did.

"To issue a challenge is to ask for the right to marry them." A bit of a giggle laced Queenie's voice. "The battle is their official bonding ceremony. And you won."

Amy's spine suddenly sparked to life, electric arcs zinging along its length and spreading over her skin. She snapped her head toward the doorway she had used to enter the cargo hold. Dorn stood there, the light gleaming off his blue skin and making his white hair seem to glow. Amy ducked down, pressing herself closer to the crates as he turned and stared in her direction. Queenie followed Amy's gaze and snickered.

"Oh look," she said. "It's your husband."

Chapter Nine

The scanners hadn't been able to pick up Amy for several minutes. Dorn might have panicked if he wasn't able to feel her through their bond. Her sense of purpose had pushed aside the fear lurking beneath her resolve, overpowering it as she worked toward her goal—to protect those she loved. The emotion was so strong, it was like a beacon for Dorn to follow.

Amy truly believed her sisters were in immediate danger from Dorn and his fellow warriors. His jaw clenched. Kral and Lar would protect Becca and Sophie with their lives. All of the warriors in their prism would do so, but it would hardly be necessary, given both women's fierceness and ability to defend themselves. Neither sister was as skilled as Amy in battle, though. Dorn's chest swelled with pride.

Amy had challenged him—and won. They were joined according to the culture of his people, though they were not fully bonded through their soulmate connection. Yet.

Even unbonded, he could feel her emotions clearly. They were softer now, as if something was making her happy. What could possibly be doing so? There was no sense of victory lacing her happiness, so she hadn't found a way off the station. She was by turns frustrated, amused, and feeling deep affection. She must have encountered someone who was helping her.

It was probably the one who had shown Amy a place on the station that the scanners couldn't reach. Luckily for Dorn, he didn't need scanners to find her. He strode down the corridor he was sure she had taken, then paused in front of the open archway that led to one of the station's cargo bays. Amy was somewhere inside. He stepped into the large space, his hopes of a quick reunion dashed when he saw the immense amount of storage items stacked throughout the hold. Amy could be hiding in so many places.

The scanners would detect her if she was among the cargo. No, she was someplace else. Someplace… higher. He sensed her watching him, preparing herself for action. At least this time, she didn't have quite the same deadly purpose behind her thoughts. He glanced around, hunting for what could have softened her edges so effectively. He might be the one needing their help when Dorn and Amy spoke again.

Surveying the room, his attention focused on the highest stack of crates at the far end of the cargo hold. Amy was there. His spine plates rose as he felt her eyes on him, arcs of pleasure traveling along his nerves. His hands ached to hold her, his hearts were pounding with need. She was his, and he would spend the rest of his life convincing her of how perfectly they fit together in all ways.

The gaps between the crates were so narrow his shoulders would brush either side if he walked between them. The crates themselves were only stacked twenty feet high nearest him, though. He coiled and leapt to the top of the crate, pausing to test his balance and their stability. They seemed to be stacked fairly well.

Amy was watching him. He felt a surge of fear and excitement flow out from her. His leap had impressed her. He could do much more than that to catch his mate's attention. He ran across the tops of the crates, leaping from one group to the next, never slowing. In seconds, he would reach her and have her in his arms. He could already almost feel her warmth pressed against him, her softness burrowing into his side.

Wait, was he imagining that feeling, or was Amy projecting something she was experiencing? Who was she with that she held so closely?

Amy was his soulmate. *His*. She was his wife. He was the one she should be holding against her chest.

He quickened his pace, even as he felt her recoil. She was afraid, but she had nothing to fear from him. He would show her just as soon as he reached her. With a final leap, he cleared an entire stack of crates and the gaps between them, ascending another thirty feet. The gravity weakened when he was within a few feet of the tall stack of crates. Without its effect slowing him down, he hurtled past his intended landing spot, sliding to a stop when his feet finally touched down on the crates' upper surface.

Amy stood before him, her eyes wide and her chest heaving with each breath. She held something against her chest. Something small and furry—white with spots of color here and there. Was that a kitten?

He had intended to land on the very edge of her hiding place, wanting to give Amy space and let her see that he meant no harm. Instead, he had barreled right up to her, invading the refuge that had helped calm her nerves. She took one look at him and all the rage he had felt from her before surged to the surface. Resolve flooded her again as she lifted her arm toward him.

"Amy, don't!"

His warning was too late, not that she would have listened to him anyway. She fired her blaster. Dorn easily blocked the energy with his shield, feet planted to absorb the impact without losing ground. He had trained in low-G combat.

Amy hadn't.

The force of the blast sent her flying back into the hull of the space station only a few feet behind her. His own skull throbbed in sympathy as hers made a loud *crack* upon impact. Her eyes fluttered shut as she slowly started to fall forward. The kitten clung to the front of her shirt, crying out, "Amy!" in a childlike, female voice. Dorn rushed forward to catch them both.

How hard had Amy hit her head? He knew that humans were fragile, but it seemed impossible that the impact could render her unconscious. His hearts sped, panic rising in him and clouding his thoughts. He had to remain calm. Amy needed him. He had to protect her, would do anything to keep her safe.

Apparently, he wasn't the only one.

"Unhand her, you… you… jerk face," the kitten yelled. She swiped at him with one of her paws, claws outstretched. They tickled as they raked across his forearm. Her other claws were still firmly gripping Amy's shirt.

"If I let go of her, she'll fall on you," Dorn said. "Is that what you want?"

The kitten looked up at Amy, then back to him. In a small voice, she said, "No."

His heart softened at the slight tremor to the kitten's tone. Dorn lifted Amy into his arms, his hearts racing as he thought back to the first time he had seen her. She had been injured then, too, and he had almost lost her. He wouldn't come close to losing her again. Her heartbeat was strong, as was his sense of her. That reassured him as he cradled her against his chest, making sure to support her neck with his elbow. The kitten hissed at him, using Amy's torso as a support to bat at Dorn's face.

"I swear by the Makers, I will find your weak spot," she growled, moving her attack to his neck.

Dorn couldn't stifle a small laugh. It was hard to believe he could make the sound when he was so terrified.

"What is your name, kitten?"

She narrowed her eyes at him and straightened, "Queenie."

"A fitting name for one so fierce."

She sniffed and turned her head to the side, but kept her gaze on him from the very corner of her eye. He'd seen similar looks from the only other kitten he had met, Patches, when she didn't want to admit interest in something. Now that he thought on it, Patches and Queenie looked very similar, except for Queenie's longer fur. Dorn strode to the edge of the crates.

"Hold on," he said.

"To what?"

"Your friend—and your fierceness."

Queenie looked over at Amy, then nodded. She curled up in the space where Amy's body pressed against Dorn's, gingerly gripping Amy's shirt with her claws. Dorn leapt across the space, landing easily on the second stack over. He could have just dropped to the floor, but he didn't want the momentum to harm either of his charges. As soon as his feet hit the crates, he ran to the edge, jumping from one stack to the other until he was near the exit. He crouched low as he leapt to the floor, letting his knees absorb the impact as much as possible to keep Amy and Queenie safe.

"Well, that was—" Queenie yelped as he bolted down the corridor, heading back to the medical bays.

His hearts were pounding so hard, he thought they would burst from his chest. He had to calm himself. Amy's heart would try to match his beat, just as his sought to match hers. He didn't know what effect that would have on her. The white hallways around him blurred as he increased his speed. He glanced down to see Queenie's eyes wide and her fur standing on end all over her body. He hated to frighten her, but didn't have time to waste.

Finally, his destination appeared. He skidded to a stop in front of the door to the medical bay where Rin was regenerating. Glancing at the access pad, he looked back to Amy. How was he going to open the door while holding her?

"Allow me." Queenie shook herself, then walked toward the panel on unsteady legs.

Dorn moved closer so that she could reach more easily. The kitten swiped at the panel, keying in a sequence that opened the door.

"How did you…" he began.

"The station's security is abysmal. Worse than the *Reckoning*, even. It's child's play, really." She cocked her head to the side and said, "Literally, I suppose."

He had never been more grateful for lax security protocols in his life. Stepping into the room, he headed straight for Rin's regen bed.

"You wouldn't happen to know how to deactivate one of these things to get the person out?" Dorn asked.

Queenie snorted, then leapt from Amy's stomach onto the glass lid of the bed. She peered inside. "We don't need to. He's coming out of it now."

Rin's eyelids fluttered and his breathing deepened. As he looked up at Queenie standing above him, his eyes grew wide and his chest heaved in rapid breaths. He pressed his hands against the sides of the regen bed, recoiling from the kitten. Queenie's ears perked forward and her whiskers twitched. She hopped to the metal at the top of the regen bed, crouching low. Rin followed her every move with his eyes, inching away from her as much as he could.

"What a peculiar Sadirian," she said. "So intriguing."

Did Rin not know about cats? It seemed the only explanation for his fear. The clear cover of the regen bed slid up and over, back into its housing when the bed wasn't in use. Rin didn't wait for it to finish docking itself before rolling out of the bed and scrambling away. He managed to spin to his feet, arms flailing to get his balance as he backed away from Queenie. She stared at him with pupils so broad, her eyes were barely gold-rimmed. Her hips wiggled as she stared at him, as if she was readying herself to attack.

"Queenie," Dorn warned.

At the same time, Rin pointed and said, "Keep that cat away from me."

"So, you do know what a cat is," Dorn said.

"I know that they're dangerous." Rin swallowed hard, eyes locked on Queenie.

"Queenie is a kitten," Dorn said. "She's a baby cat."

"Excuse me, I am not a baby," Queenie said, indignantly.

Rin's eyes grew even wider. "Holy fuck, she can talk."

Queenie blinked and sat up, her pupils narrowing. "I can, but I choose not to use such vulgar language."

"Wha…" Rin shook his head, then ran a hand over his face. "What?"

"Vulgar. Language." Queenie bit out each word. "I'm not a baby, but I'm still… young." She glared at Rin. "That kind of language isn't appropriate."

"I…" Rin shook his head again. His shoulders lowered a bit, but tension still radiated from his stance. "I suppose so. I apologize."

"That's more like it," she said.

"I don't care how you talk," Dorn said. "I just want you to heal my wife."

"Wife?" Rin finally looked away from Queenie. He glanced at Amy and backed away again. "Oh no. You've got to be kidding me."

"I am deadly serious." Dorn gently placed Amy in the regen bed, then smoothed a few strands of her dark hair away from her forehead. "She hit her head in the cargo hold hard enough to knock herself out."

Rin cautiously approached, looking back and forth between Queenie and Amy.

"Do you always surround yourself with such dangerous women?" Rin said.

Queenie's eyes softened as she turned her head away and flicked her tail indifferently. Dorn could tell the statement pleased her, though. He reached out and scratched the top of her head.

"I wouldn't have it any other way," he said.

Queenie chuffed, then leapt onto his shoulder. Dorn took the opportunity to step further away from the regen bed. Though he hated to leave Amy's side, he didn't think Rin would approach if there were two threats so close. Rin circled around them as far as he could to get to Amy, then began tapping commands onto the side of the regen bed. A holographic image of Amy floated above her, a section of her brain highlighted with flashing light.

"She has a mild concussion," Rin said. "Nothing they couldn't treat even on Earth. Minor bruising of her chin and slight burns around her wrists as well."

Dorn's hearts ached with each addition to his soulmate's—his wife's—injuries. Cygnians were born to battle, but they were more physically resilient than Earthlings. Part of him thought he should have protected her better. Another knew that she would have kicked his ass even harder if she knew he was thinking such a thing.

"She only needs a few minutes in the regen bed, then she'll be right as rain." Under his breath, Rin added, "Or at least, as right as she ever was."

Dorn let out a breath that seemed to hollow him out. He was almost dizzy with relief. Queenie butted her head against his cheek, a soothing, rumbling vibration coming from her chest. Dorn reached up and petted her gently, gratified when she pressed her tiny form into his palm.

"Take care of her," Dorn said. "There are people I need to contact."

Chapter Ten

Amy was lying down on a firm bed again. She blinked her eyes open and found herself once more staring at a plain white ceiling lit with overly bright lights. A gorgeous blue face framed with snow-white hair entered her field of vision, looking down at her. Queenie was perched on his shoulder, head cocked to the side.

"Look who's here," Queenie said, her tone filled with mirth. "It's your husband."

Amy rolled her eyes shut briefly and murmured, "Balls."

"I understand your sentiment," Dorn arched an eyebrow, then raised one of his enormous hands to block Queenie's view. "But seriously. You shouldn't talk that way in front of the kitten."

Amy's teeth ground together hard enough to make a clacking noise. She was going to kill them both. Okay, not Queenie, but definitely Dorn. Maybe Dorn. Okay, maybe she wasn't going to kill anyone, but she was definitely going to find a way to get back at them for enjoying her predicament. She rolled to her side, swatting Dorn's hands away when he reached for her. Swinging her legs over the bed's edge on the opposite side to where he was standing, she took a moment, stabilizing herself with her arms. The room spun a bit, but quickly righted itself.

She closed her eyes and breathed in and out for a few moments. When she opened them again, a handsome man stood before her. His eyes were dark and warm and his straight black hair slicked back from his face. He was absolutely built, which she could easily see from the skin-tight silver catsuit he was wearing. She bristled, scooting away from him as he approached. She wasn't quite sure she could stand yet.

"This is Rin," Dorn said. "He's your doctor."

"Nice uniform." Amy accented each word, pushing as much threat into her eyes as she could.

"Thanks?" Rin glanced at Dorn in confusion.

"The Tau Ceti who originally attacked Amy were disguised as Coalition soldiers," Dorn said, his voice tight and low. "Three of them abducted her sister and left Amy for dead."

A wave of rage flowed out from him like a tsunami. Amy gasped as it hit her, making all the hairs on her arms stand on end. Her spine lit up with enough energy, she almost felt as though it could lift her off the bed and to her feet, the electric arcs pulsing down her arms and legs, readying her for battle.

"You okay?" Rin asked, angling his head so he could

see her face better. He was tall, but within human range, not like Dorn or Kral.

"Yeah." She glared at Dorn over her shoulder. "Somebody just needs to chill." She looked back at Rin and added, "And everyone needs to give me space."

Rin straightened, leveling an even stare at Amy. The pinched skin around the corners of his eyes betrayed his own anger.

"I believe there's an Earth phrase, 'one good turn deserves another,'" Rin said. "Well, one *bad* turn does *not* deserve another. My people didn't attack you. *I* didn't attack you. Dorn and his prism saved you and I've been doing my damnedest to figure out what's going on with your shoulder and set you right. And you almost killed me, along with Dorn."

Oh shit. Was he one of the soldiers that she had attacked earlier?

"Sorry," she said. She meant it. Kind of. But she could barely convince *herself* of her sincerity. Rin didn't seem to be buying it at all.

Rin was quiet for a moment, lines of strain deepening at the corners of his eyes, then said, "What has Dorn told you about the war?"

"What war?" Dread rose in her as scenario after scenario ran through her mind. Aliens were active on or around earth and somehow her family was involved. Anything was possible.

Rin cast a quick glare at Dorn, then crossed his arms over his own impressive chest. “The galactic war that you and your family have managed to stumble into.”

Her stomach clenched and the hairs on her arms stood on end. She did not like the sound of that at all.

“We haven’t had much of a chance to talk yet,” she said.

“She was busy attacking me,” Dorn said, a fierce joy radiating from him. What the hell was up with him?

Oh right. Because she had fought him and kicked his ass, they were married now. She still wasn’t sure she believed in soulmates, but she *did* believe in marriage. There were enough cultural idiosyncrasies between countries on Earth that she could understand how she’d totally stepped in it with her first interaction with Dorn by not knowing more about his people.

When she half-turned again to glare at him, he had the gall to smile at her. A wave of warmth flowed out from him, wrapping around her like a comfortable blanket and sinking all the way into her bones. His eyes softened, the irises glowing a vibrant green. Damn, he was gorgeous. And he was her husband, apparently. His lips quirked up at one side as she kept staring at him. The warmth amped up to heat that sent prickles of pleasure all along her back and chest, spreading through her belly and flooding her core.

Smug bastard.

“Stop that,” she snapped. She turned back to Rin,

determined to ignore Dorn, and said, "Give me the rundown."

"Ugh, so boring." Queenie rolled her eyes and let out a comically exaggerated yawn. "If you're going to be giving a history lesson, I'm going to find something more exciting to do."

Rin glared at her. "Like sabotaging the station's systems?"

She chuffed, then ran down Dorn's arm and leapt to the regen bed. "Relax, Sadirian. This station is built with Vegan technology. It isn't as easy to manipulate as what you have on the *Reckoning*."

"That's only mildly reassuring." Rin stepped back as she jumped to the floor.

Queenie ran to the door, then leapt up, batting at the panel next to it. As soon as her paws hit the floor, the door opened.

"Later, human," she said.

Rin let out a breath, visibly relaxing as the kitten left. There was definitely a story there—maybe several—but Amy didn't let herself get distracted. She needed information.

"You were saying," Amy prompted.

Rin nodded, then said, "My people are called Sadirians. Genetically, we're almost identical to humans. Until recently, we were governed by a High Council with… I would say, 'questionable morals,' but there's no question to it. They were corrupt, and you would most likely consider them outright evil. I would tend to agree."

Dorn seemed to agree as well. A chill crashed through her as Dorn's warmth vanished. Amy missed it despite herself, a strange sensation rising up in her as if she was reaching for him even though she held her body still.

Soulmates, huh?

She shook the thought away, not ready to face it yet. This whole 'galactic war' thing seemed a lot more important. She'd figure out what was going on between herself and Dorn later.

"This isn't helping my view of you guys in silver suits," Amy said.

"It shouldn't," Rin said. "There are Sadirians you need to be careful of. The High Council used regen beds like this one to mentally program us without our knowing about it. They could make us think, feel, even remember whatever they wanted us to."

Amy jumped to her feet, turning to stare at the seemingly innocuous bed. "And you put me in one of them?"

"This unit only repairs the physical body," Dorn said, a wave of fierce protectiveness flowing off of him. "I would never have let them put you in it otherwise."

She was only vaguely mollified.

"We're trying to identify people who still have dangerous programming or are just holding on to the old ways for whatever reason," Rin said.

"Psychological comfort or personal gain," Amy murmured, rubbing her arms as she stepped farther away from the regen bed.

Rin nodded. "Which are really one and the same."

Her frown deepened. She was starting to like this guy. No way she would trust him yet, but she could appreciate his perspective.

"I'm guessing somebody took them out," Amy said. "The High Council. Was it an internal rebellion?"

She kind of doubted that, if they were controlling their populace that much. The thought was terrifying.

"Not exactly." The warm undertones of Rin's skin paled as he went on, increasing Amy's misgivings. "The High Council created what we call the Coalition of Planets. It expands across most of our galaxy. The majority of the systems in the Coalition are colony worlds settled by Sadirians. The others are made up of alien sentients who had various degrees of enthusiasm about joining us."

"But, they weren't given a choice," Amy concluded.

Rin nodded. Behind her, Dorn exuded a near constant wave of disapproval, bordering on contempt. He seemed to like Rin well enough, but this little history lesson was bringing out a lot of anger in Dorn. If what Rin was saying was true, Amy understood.

"Two systems have banded together and split from the Coalition," Rin said. "The Centaurans and the Tau Ceti."

His voice hitched at the mention of the latter aliens, a haunted look entering his eyes. "They call themselves the Tau Centauran Assembly."

"And they aren't much better than the High Council?" Amy asked.

"The Centaurans have always been peaceful, but the Tau Ceti…" Rin shook his head. "They are a violent, destructive people. The first act of the Assembly was to utterly destroy our homeworld, Sadr-4, as well as all the colony planets and space stations in our home system. The High Council was on Sadr-4 when it detonated. Since then, the Assembly has made a point of destroying every new colony we've tried to establish outside of the Sol system and many of our pre-existing colonies. If they take over, the galaxy will become a much darker place."

Amy didn't want to ask, but forced herself. "Worse than total mind control?"

"Much, much worse," Rin said. "Somehow, they've gotten their hands on technology that rivals that of our most advanced allies."

"And those are?" Amy asked. "I want specifics."

If she didn't have all the data, how could she form a plan that would protect her loved ones—and her entire freaking planet? The concept overwhelmed her mind, bringing back the dizziness from when she had just woken up. She pushed away the thought and resultant anxiety, keeping her focus on gathering as much information as she could.

"The Vegans," Dorn said. He stepped around the bed so that he could stand beside her. "They're a small, bipedal reptilian species from the Vega system. Each is outfitted with an exosuit, which appear as silver bands over their bodies, but can morph into pretty much whatever they need."

"The Vegans have allied themselves with Earth, so your homeworld is fairly protected," Rin said. "The only reason our new colonies in the Sol system are safe is because the Vegans have placed this entire system under their protection. Earth's Department of Homeworld Security has given us permission to be here, so the Vegans extended their protection to us as well."

Rin's dark eyes glittered. "If it weren't for them, my people wouldn't have any hope of survival or ever having homes again. The war isn't…" His voice became raspy, and he coughed to clear his throat. "It isn't going well for us."

Amy's heart ached for him. She wished she couldn't imagine what that would be like for his people, but she had researched too much of her own planet's history, thinking through situations and how she might handle them. Her eyes hurt, her temples starting to throb. She rubbed them absently. All that training she had done had not prepared her for something on this scale. How could she keep her family safe in the midst of this?

"How is my family involved?" Amy asked. "Why were we attacked?"

"Even with their advanced technology, the Assembly doesn't stand a chance against the Vegans," Dorn said. "They wanted to bring my people into the war on their side."

"So, Cygnians aren't part of the Coalition?" Amy asked.

Dorn snorted, contempt rolling off him in clear waves. "Never."

"Their homeworld is right next to the black hole Earthlings call Cygnus X-3," Rin said. "Our ships can't go near their system without imploding from the gravitational forces."

Dorn grinned, the light glimmering off his sharp teeth. Were they serrated? She leaned forward for a closer look. He caught her staring and smirked again. She jerked back, glaring at him as she parsed through what she'd learned. Or at least, what they wanted her to think.

"We were targeted because of this soulmate thing," Amy said.

Dorn's eyebrows rose and his lips parted in surprise. More heat flooded her, approval, appreciation, and a hefty dose of desire lighting her up. If he was playing her, he was doing a masterful job of it. His expressions backed up the emotions she kept feeling from him. It was so tempting to take him at his word.

"That's right," Dorn said. Amy could feel the strain in him as he tried to clamp down his emotions when he continued. "A Tau Ceti triad was sent disguised as Sadirians with the intention of taking Becca, killing one of you, and leaving the other alive as a witness. Becca was to be killed at a later time and her body planted on the *Reckoning*—the Coalition warship stationed in the Sol system to provide additional protection to the Sadirians living here."

"What about the fourth man?" Amy asked. "The one who…" She shook her head, trying to remember him clearly.

He had appeared human at first, claiming that he was their friend Hayley's ex-boyfriend and that she was in trouble. Amy had been distracted by the three men who had attacked her, but the fourth… He was the one who had taken Sophie. Amy had a vague memory of his arms changing shape, becoming almost like gleaming tentacles that wrapped around her sister.

"I wondered if you had seen him," Dorn said. "The fourth was a shapeshifting mercenary from the Scorpii system. He calls himself Dean."

Shapeshifting mercenary… That explained what he'd done with his arms. A shiver passed over her that had nothing to do with Dorn's presence.

"Dean was involved in the abduction?" Rin's face became almost bloodless, his eyes widening as he took a step back. He shook his head as he looked Amy up and down. "I continue to underestimate you. Not many people survive an encounter with a Scorpiian who wants them dead."

"One of the Tau Ceti soldiers threw off the other's aim," Amy said. "Or else I *would* be dead."

"His name is Tobek," Dorn said. "He's a double agent who helped us rescue Sophie and tried to prevent your injury, but failed. His mission was to protect you all." Dorn's lips pulled from his teeth in a threatening grimace.

She would have to thank Tobek for saving her life if she ever met him. And then kick his ass for not doing a better job protecting her sisters.

For a few moments, Amy let herself process everything she'd learned. The Tau Ceti strategy was brilliant and would have worked if Tobek hadn't messed with their plans. The missing pieces had fallen into place. So much made sense to her now.

Dorn hadn't abducted her. Neither had Kral and Lar abducted Becca and Sophie. The relief Amy felt made her giddy—not just that they were safe, but that Dorn wasn't a 'bad guy,' as Queenie would say. Warmth flowed through Amy as she turned to look at Dorn, and this time she didn't fight it.

"So, you recruited Tobek?" she asked. "Even though he's a Tau Ceti?"

"Yes." Dorn answered too quickly. A sharp spike of

dread and guilt surged through him.

Amy narrowed her eyes. "What aren't you telling me?"

"A great deal," Dorn said. "But the rest is not something I can share in front of a Sadirian."

Amy bristled on Rin's behalf. She knew she was only just getting a grasp on all the different factions and alliances, but Rin had had a pretty rough time of it, and she hadn't made things any easier on him when she had attacked him. She was pretty sure she had broken some of his ribs with that kick.

Rin lifted his hands and shook his head. "As long as whatever you say doesn't set her off again, that's fine. I have other duties anyway." He turned to Amy and said, "If you need me—"

"She won't," Dorn cut in.

"Don't be a dick," Amy said. She turned back to Rin. "How do I access the station's communication system if I need you?"

"There are panels along the walls at regular intervals," he said. "Place your hand on one and say, 'Contact Rin,' and that will connect you."

"Thanks."

Rin nodded slightly, then headed for the exit. The door slid open, then shut behind him. As soon as he was gone, Amy became aware of her mistake in not asking him to stay. She looked up at Dorn, heat flooding through her as she realized they were alone.

Chapter Eleven

The green glow of Dorn's eyes intensified. Motes of rainbow light sparked around them like embers from a downed power line. Amy could feel his heat wrapping around her, his desire rolling from him in palpable waves along with a deeper emotion. An emotion she wasn't ready to name, but that stoked a corresponding response from her.

Something inside of her shifted. An energy she'd never experienced. Her skin buzzed with it, goosebumps rising all along her arms and back. The energy surged toward Dorn, pulling her along with it. Her feet shuffled forward, her neck tilting back so that she could keep looking into those amazing green eyes, so that she could get closer to him. As close as she could.

Why did she want this? Want him? It was all so impossible. *He* was impossible. Yet there he was right in front of her, wanting her, *yearning* for her. Her soulmate. She still wasn't sure she even believed in souls. At least, she never had before. The more time she spent with Dorn, the more she wondered.

He lifted his hand toward her face. She should leap out

of reach, but knew she wouldn't. Her breath quickened, her heart racing in anticipation of his touch.

"Amy."

Her name alone on his lips sent a jolt of pleasure through her. Her toes curled in her sneakers, the constant surge of energy racing up and down her spine built to lightning. His knuckle grazed along the edge of her jaw, a whisper of a touch that felt like a nuke detonating deep in her belly, heat flooding her core and making her clench with need. At this rate, she wouldn't even need a warm-up to be ready for him.

The effect he had on her was too intense. It wasn't normal. But then again, she was married to an alien. What part of her life was normal anymore?

"Your new injuries have been healed," he said. "How do you feel?"

Amy's mouth was suddenly dry. She swallowed a few times to make sure her voice would be strong when she spoke.

"Strange," she said. "I'm not injured that I can tell, but all these goosebumps are freaking me out."

She hadn't meant to share that much, but it was so easy to talk to him. He was too easy to trust—and way too easy to desire.

"It's the soulmate bond," he said. "Our bodies will continue to feel a pull toward each other until we achieve unity."

"Unity?" She did not like the sound of that. Images from sci-fi horror movies played through her mind. As hot as Dorn was, she wasn't about to fuse with him.

"We will retain our individuality," he said, rushing to reassure her. Concern washed over her, a deep anxiety threading through his emotions. "Unity refers to the experience of our souls temporarily merging—two distinct halves coming together in a brief moment of ecstasy."

Amy arched an eyebrow. "That sounds like sex."

He smirked, his anxiety fading as desire took its place. Her face heated, along with other parts of her body. Hadn't he said something about more than one dick earlier? How the hell would that work? She was more curious than she wanted to admit.

"Unity is achieved through mating," Dorn said. "Once we have reached the state, it will be easier for us to read each other's emotions and locate each other when needed."

"Like you found me in the cargo bay."

He nodded. Amy walked back to the regen bed, mulling over the information he had given her. She needed space to clear her head. Except the farther she was from him, the more her thoughts clouded. That pull was growing stronger, filling her head with images of the pair of them tangled together, a sheen of sweat on their bodies.

Did he even sweat? How could she be contemplating this when she barely knew anything about him?

Being able to read his emotions more clearly could be

useful, but he would gain the same advantage. They were already married. Tying herself even more closely to him didn't seem like a smart idea. Then again, maybe binding him closer would work out in her favor. Surely he would side with her—his wife—over his friends if it came to that.

She was reaching. Grasping at straws trying to justify what she already knew she wanted. Him. She braced her hands on the firm surface of the bed and closed her eyes.

Go through the scenarios. Think of potential eventualities.

She felt him approach even though he hadn't made a sound. His heat was right behind her. She could lean back and fall into it. Into him.

"Amy." Again, the word flooded her with heat.

Goosebumps raced along her skin, her nipples hardened, her core ached with need. He ran his hands along her arms, barely touching her, yet lighting up her nerves like a summer storm.

"Sometimes you can't figure things out with your mind," he said. "There is no strategy to be contemplated here. There is only you and me and the bond between us."

She stood straighter, bringing her back into contact with his chest. The lightning pleasure running along her spine intensified, an echoing sensation flowing through her from him. She could feel the currents synchronizing, the strong beat of two hearts reverberating through her shoulders from both sides of his rib cage.

"Can you read my mind now?" she asked. His words had been uncannily accurate.

He knew her. Knew her soul-deep. Was she a fool to think that she knew him, too?

"Not yet." He chuckled, the sound vibrating through her muscle and bone, making her gasp and lean against him harder. He gripped her arms gently, his thumbs dusting across her skin. "After many decades, we may have the good fortune of our bond deepening enough for us to share our thoughts at our choosing. Until then, we'll have to muddle through with only our emotions and words to guide us."

She could think of worse guides in this new reality. She had to admit, Dorn had handled things the way she would have if their roles were reversed. His actions had been strategic, but she felt his kindness and desire underlying everything he had done. Not desire for her physically, though that was there. He wanted her to be happy. Or, he was damn good at fooling her.

What was that saying? 'The best way out is through?' Amy knew she was too far down this path to turn back, too close to Dorn to turn away. The moment she admitted it to herself, the truth became clear. She didn't want to.

Amy turned in his arms, her brown eyes wide with an

emotion he hadn't sensed from her before now. She was nervous, but also excited. Her pupils grew larger, her lips parted on a breath she took and held. She reached up to cup his cheek with her hand. The light dusting of her fingertips as they drew along his skin sent a jolt through his body, but it was nothing next to the blast flooding him with heat as she pressed her palm to his face and drew him down to her.

He bent to her eagerly, not hesitating as he captured her lips with his. They were softer than he could have ever imagined. She gasped, opening to him as his tongue plunged into her mouth. For a moment, she seemed suspended, as if she was uncertain of what to do, but then she buried her fingers in his hair, pulling herself closer and deepening the kiss. Her tongue sparred with his as skillfully as they had fought earlier. Her nails raked along his scalp, sending shockwaves of sensation through him.

Dorn lifted her so that she was sitting on the regen bed, then gripped her thighs and urged her to wrap her legs around his hips. She moaned, tightening her grip on his hair as he ground his dicks against her core. He wanted to take his time with her, to learn her body, but the desperate need to claim her as his mate tore at his self-control.

He slid his hands beneath her shirt, feeling her heated skin beneath his palms. Without stopping, he reached up to her small breasts, palming each in his hands. She moaned again as he rubbed her tight nipples, pinching them between his fingertips. Everything about her was perfect. She was the missing half of his universe, and they were about to be made whole.

He started to press her onto the flat surface of the regen bed, but she pushed at him, urging him to give her space. There was no regret in her emotion or change in her desire. He leaned back, confused about what she needed, desperate to give her everything he had.

"Naked," she said with panting breaths. "Get naked. Now."

He let out a laugh and shook his head, relief coursing through him. Even feeling her emotions, he hadn't been certain whether she still wanted to complete their bond. Her mind was always working, and he had no doubt she would restrain herself if she thought it was the right thing to do. Stepping back, he began undoing the laces of his tunic. He undressed more quickly than he ever had in his life.

Amy removed her own clothes with a similar speed, throwing them in a pile on the floor. He tried not to let the sight of her distract him—the dusky beaded nipples on her breasts, the soft curls at the apex of her legs. The sight of her lithe body gleaming in the light was enough to make him stumble as he removed his boots.

She laughed, then crossed her arms over her chest. "Step it up," she ordered. "Come on, let's go."

He laughed again at her enthusiasm and the playful

tinge to the emotions that continuously flowed toward him. Desire dominated everything. She wanted him as badly as he wanted her. He would not disappoint her. Rising after dealing with his boots, he hooked his thumbs in his waistband and slid his pants down his legs, keeping his eyes on her face the entire time. He would remember her expression for the rest of his life.

Her eyes grew huge as his erections were freed, her mouth dropping open and her arms falling to her sides. He stepped out of his pants, smirking as she kept staring, her gaze traveling down his muscled legs, then back up again with another long pause at his dicks. Her desire was building as she stared at him. He wished he could see into her mind already. What was she thinking as she stared at him that had her nearly melting with need?

She was enjoying his appearance so much. He wanted to build on that, to stoke her desire for him till it burned hotter than a plasma core. He wanted her as desperate for him as he was for her.

"Do you like what you see?" he asked, his voice low and husky.

Slowly, he reached down and gripped one of his dicks in each of his hands, watching as her eyes grew even wider. He imagined it was her hands on him as he gave them a long stroke, pleasure heating through his muscles at the thought of pushing her back on the regen bed and claiming her as his own. Her desire exploded like a supernova, the heat of it blasting through him.

She looked up at him, eyes alight with need, and said, “You need to fuck me right now.”

He all but leapt forward, grabbing her up against his chest and lifting her from the ground. She wrapped her legs around his waist, clutching him to her as she kissed him with a passion that bordered on ferocity. Tightening her grip with her legs, she brought her sex to his larger, primary dick. His chest nearly exploded from the pleasure of her wet heat, the silken sheath tantalizingly close. But he wouldn’t hurt her and she couldn’t be ready for him.

He reached between them, easily holding her up with one arm, and ran the backs of his knuckles along her slit, gathering her wetness before swirling his fingertips over her clit. She groaned, digging her fingers into his shoulders as he slid two fingers deep into her core, his thumb still circling her most sensitive spot. She threw her head back, crying out. His dicks were throbbing, aching with the need to fill her, but he had to be sure. He spread his fingers, stretching her, pumping them within her body, pulling as much pleasure from her as he could.

“Please,” she moaned. “Dorn, please.”

A rush swept through him strong enough to take his breath away. This incredible woman, this force of nature stronger than any he had ever known, was begging him to claim her. He could feel her need as strong as his own. It was more than he could stand. He lifted his mating cock, letting his secondary dick press against her entrance. He was still worried about causing her pain from its size and held himself back, trying to ease into her. A burst of frustration hit him from Amy—his only warning before she tightened her legs and drew herself down, impaling herself on his shaft.

She screamed, her pleasure coursing through him as an orgasm racked her body. His control snapped as her silken skin pulsed around him. He gripped her hips, pounding into her tight sheath. His primary dick rubbed along her clit with each powerful stroke, sending her higher into her own bliss. Pressure built within him, faster than he could have dreamed, erupting in the most intense orgasm he had ever experienced. Each wave of pleasure crashed through him, lighting up every cell in his body, preparing him for unity.

He couldn't wait. Still pulsing, he let his secondary dick slide from her body. She was only just beginning to relax against him, her eyes closed and a soft smile on her lips, as he lined up his primary dick and rammed into her. Amy reacted instantly, her eyes snapping open and her hands grabbing his shoulders as she met his passion equally once more.

She was heaven. She was everything.

Her body invited him in, her core so tight and hot. Lost in the arcs of pleasure still coursing through him, he pounded into her over and over. His hearts followed hers, their cadence growing closer to a single beat. He leaned her back over the regen bed, pressing his body against hers, using one hand to lift her thigh so that he could drive himself deeper. She angled her hips, rocking against him in time with his thrusts, her back arching against the bed. She drew her nails down his back, digging them in when she reached his backside, urging him on.

Near crazed with need, his vision began to blur, his spine plates vibrating so strongly, the metal of the bed frame resonated from it. The lightning building in him exploded as Amy brought up her hands and ran them along the plates on each side. She cried out his name, writhing beneath him as he drove himself into her over and over, landing as deeply as he could. Eyes clenched shut, he threw his head back and roared as his mating cock spilled itself inside of her, pinning her to the bed with his final thrust.

She held him tightly, still surprising him with her strength, both of them gasping for breath. At last, his hearts beat in perfect synchronicity with hers. Her grip relaxed, and she ran her hands along his back in a gentle stroke that both soothed and aroused him further, his secondary dick already stirring again.

Dorn finally opened his eyes to see rainbows all around them. Amy was staring up at him, a soft smile on her face. In that moment, he didn't think he had ever been so at peace.

Chapter Twelve

"Unity, huh?" Amy said, her entire body liquid relaxation.

She had wanted to be able to sense his emotions. Hell, if she was honest with herself, she was looking forward to riding those amazing dicks of his—which did not disappoint. But she hadn't realized how intense the experience of bonding with him would really be. Or, how fulfilling.

It was like a huge part of her that she hadn't even known was missing had suddenly fallen into place. No big fuss. No worries or strategies needed. Being with Dorn was as effortless as breathing.

"Unity." He nodded, then angled his head, looking at more of the rainbows surrounding them. A sense of wonder emanated from him as clear and crisp as sunlight on a spring morning. "I had heard the stories, but didn't think it would be so beautiful."

"What would?"

He turned back to her and said, "The rainbows."

She glanced around them. "There are a lot more of them than usual."

Dorn's brow furrowed. "More than usual? You've seen rainbows like this before?"

"Yeah. I've seen them around you the whole time. I mean, not this dramatic or anything, but they're always there."

His lips quirked up in a small smile. "You can see the colors on your wristbands, can't you?"

She arched an eyebrow at him. "How else do you think I kicked your ass?"

He laughed, letting his chin fall toward his chest. Damn, even his forehead was sexy. She had it bad for this guy. She was only reassured by being able to feel that he had it just as bad for her. The way he felt when he looked at her made her toes curl. Like she was the most precious thing in the universe.

"Remarkable," he said. "Not even Cygnians can perceive the lights of unity until they've achieved it."

"Maybe I was just seeing soulmate sparkles."

He laughed again, a deep, rich sound that echoed through her, the vibrations of it stimulating her in more ways than one, since his dick was still buried deep within. She could feel him growing soft inside her, but his other dick was prodding the flesh of her backside.

This could be very interesting.

As if sensing her desire—who was she kidding? He was absolutely sensing her desire—he slid from her, but only to make way for his now fully-erect second dick. He thrust into her as smooth as silk, somehow stretching her to her limits, yet not making her uncomfortable at all. The only real limits he was pushing her past were the ones she thought she had around pleasure.

Every cell in her body thrummed as he rocked against her, slowly this time. Languidly.

"We're lucky we didn't activate the regen bed's escape pod function," Dorn said, kissing the skin below her ear.

"These things are escape pods, too?"

"It's one of the few things the Coalition did right in their designs." He nuzzled her neck, giving her a long, deep stroke with his dick. "If their soldiers are unconscious within during extreme events, the pods are programmed to jettison from the ship or station they're built into."

"Then we are lucky we didn't get jettisoned," she said, laughing. "Because that was about the most extreme event I've ever been part of."

Dorn laughed, then gripped her hips and shifted her closer, deepening his strokes, but keeping them gentler than before. Their bonding had been more intense than anything she had ever experienced. Her mind was still trying to wrap itself around everything. For once, she just let it go, her thoughts trailing off as she focused instead on the pleasure Dorn was giving her, the way her spine pulsed in time with his movements, the way she could feel his hearts beating in time with her own.

"Amy," he murmured, nuzzling her neck before grazing it with his sharp teeth then kissing the spot.

She let her eyes roll shut, warmth flowing through her at the sound of her name on his lips. She had never felt like someone's 'everything' before. It was a heady thing. Addictive. Just like the feel of him buried within her. Her plan to use his emotions to sort through her situation might have backfired. Then again, it might have succeeded beyond her wildest imaginings.

Dorn was her soulmate. She became more sure of it with each touch, each word, each thrust of his shaft deep inside her. This was her husband, and they would spend the rest of their lives together. Instead of frightening her, the thought made her happy. Happier than she had ever been.

He smiled as he leaned back so that he could look into her eyes, his hips still pressing and pulling in their rhythmic motion. Subtle heat uncoiled in her, building slowly this time, letting her connect with every spark of pleasure. He leaned down and kissed her, running his hand along her thigh as he finished a particularly long stroke with his dick.

"What are you thinking that's making you so happy?" he asked.

She ran her fingers along his cheek, marveling at how beautiful he was, how brightly his eyes shone as he looked down at her.

"I'm thinking how incredible it is that we found our way to each other and to this moment, even after everything that has happened between us." After a pause, she added, "And that I'm glad we did."

He smiled, then reached up to grasp her hand, pulling it from his face so he could press a kiss against her palm. He brought it to his chest, spreading it above his right heart.

"My hearts beat for you now," he said. "For as long as I live, I am yours."

"I…" Her heartbeat picked up, and she knew he could feel it. He shared it, shared everything she experienced, just as she would for him. Her throat tightened, but she forced herself to see the truth right in front of her. The miraculous, amazing truth. "I'm yours as well."

His expression softened and another wave of warmth flowed through her. It took her a moment to figure out what he was feeling. Dear god, he loved her. With everything he was. She had never felt so… complete. Her chest was over full, her body buzzing with a pleasure that went beyond the physical. She was starting to love him, too. How could she not? He held the other half of her soul.

Souls were real. *Soulmates* were real. And aliens. It was too much to process. She drew him down to kiss her again, losing herself in the waves of pleasure spreading out from where they were joined.

Amy couldn't believe she wasn't sore. After all that 'bonding,' she shouldn't be able to walk in a straight line. But she felt invigorated, her body filled with energy. She would use it to deal with whatever came next, to sort through whatever Dorn still needed to tell her and face it together. The door slid open just as she was pulling down her shirt. She turned around and felt the blood drain from her face.

Okay, maybe she wasn't ready to face *this*.

Buddy rushed into the room, wearing one of the silver catsuit space uniforms. Amy would have laughed, except his expression was so filled with concern, she didn't have the heart to tease him about it. Yet.

"Oh my God, Amy," he said. "Are you okay?"

He pulled her into a huge hug. For some reason, her eyes filled with tears. This was her big brother. He had always made her feel safe enough to let down her guard, but she didn't want to do so in front of Dorn. Sniffing, she pushed away from Buddy and stepped back.

"I'm fine," Amy said.

"Fine?" Buddy's eyebrows rose over his steel-gray eyes. He turned his attention to Dorn, fury building in his expression. "Word is that you faced Dorn in combat. *Combat*."

"And kicked his ass," she added, smirking.

Buddy acted as if he didn't hear her. "What the fuck

were you thinking, man? She just came out of stasis after that blaster wound. She needs to be resting."

"It's okay," Amy said.

"Okay?" Buddy turned back to her, his gray eyes cold with rage. She had never seen him look at her that way before. Other people, yeah, but never her. A chill of misgiving ran down her spine. "Do you know what it means when you challenge a Cygnian to combat and win?"

"I do now," Amy said.

"Amy has accepted our union," Dorn said. "She is my soulmate."

"Soulmate." Buddy ran his hand over his face and shook his head. "I'm sick of you guys and your soulmate garbage."

"Hey." Amy couldn't believe how much she was bristling when only an hour or so ago she would have been agreeing with Buddy. "It's not garbage. It's true."

Buddy's eyebrows hiked up again. "Really? You're buying into this party line now?"

"Buddy…" she began.

"No, no," Buddy said. "This is good. Since he's explained everything and all, I'm sure he's told you all the other important stuff. Like that Sophie has been permanently altered with some sort of freaky electrical powers because of bonding with Lar. Dorn here, he told you that, right?"

Now was probably not the best time to tell Buddy that Amy had been altered as well, though she wasn't sure it had anything to do with Dorn. When her brother was this worked up, it was hard to derail him until he hit someone, and if he went for Dorn, Buddy would probably break his hand.

"Dorn has told me the most important stuff," Amy said. "I'm going into this with open eyes."

"The most important stuff?" Buddy nodded, but she could tell he was building up to something. "Did he tell you that your house blew up? Or that Hayley's been kidnapped and we have no idea where she is or if she's okay?"

Amy felt as if the floor had fallen out from under her. Hayley was missing? How could Dorn not have opened with that? She turned to him, feeling her anger welling up inside of her, but trying not to let it burst forth.

"I told you we had much to discuss," Dorn said. "There were other, more pressing matters."

"You mean matters of pressing," she quipped. "That… sounded different in my head."

"Wait a minute. Wait a minute. Excuse me?" Buddy took a step closer to Dorn, his shoulders hunched and his hands curling into fists.

This would not end well.

He glanced over at Dorn, then back to Amy. Shifting his weight, he started to pace. She hadn't seen him act like this for a long time. Not since before he had started his restaurant business, when he had what could only be described as 'anger issues.' But why the relapse? It wasn't like him. Buddy shook his head, then launched himself at Dorn, fists raised.

"She's my baby sister, man," Buddy yelled. "How could you?"

Amy leapt between them, pushing Buddy back with her left arm as gently as she could. Even pulling her punch, he flew back several feet. When he found his balance, he stared at her, his face a mask of confusion as he rubbed his chest.

"Amy?" he said. "Oh god. You, too?"

"We don't have time for this bullshit," Amy said. "If Hayley is missing, we need to work together, not fight each other. The longer she's gone, the harder it will be to find her."

Dread and sadness flowed out from Dorn. Amy turned to face him, her cheeks prickling with anxiety.

"What?" Amy said.

Dorn took a deep breath and held it for a moment, then said, "She's been gone for months."

Chapter Thirteen

Amy shook her head. "No. No, I saw her a couple of weeks ago."

"You saw the shapeshifter," Dorn said. "The Scorpiian. As near as we can tell, he targeted Hayley as soon as he learned of Kral's interest in Becca. Dean took her during her trip to Europe."

"No," Amy said, backing away from him.

So much time had passed. It would be bad enough to work a case that had been overlooked for so long if they were limited to Earth. Hayley had been taken by an alien. She could be anywhere in the universe. She could be—

Amy shook her head sharply, her stomach roiling. She refused to let her mind go down that path. She tried to remember what had happened the night she had been attacked. Any detail that might help. She had been focused on the three men in silver catsuits—the ones like what Buddy was wearing. She hadn't really looked at Dean after his lackeys had joined them, so all she had to go on was the brief glimpse she'd had as he and Sophie interacted just after he arrived.

He was wearing an expensive suit. Dark colors with a

crisp white shirt. His hair stuck up in a style that was a bit dated. His looks were chiseled, his body lean. Sophie would have been drooling over him if she hadn't been worried about Hayley. He had told them Hayley was in trouble, and Sophie had believed him. Hell, Amy had believed him, too. The strain in his voice, his eyes, his bearing, it had all seemed so sincere. Amy had believed that he cared about Hayley. How convincing was this guy?

"He posed as her ex-boyfriend," Amy said.

"He *was* her boyfriend," Buddy snapped. He waved his hand and said, "All that matters is that Hayley's been taken and we need to get her back."

Amy's brow furrowed. Something about Buddy's statement was off.

She expected him to be upset. As Hayley's surrogate 'big brother,' he was just as protective of her as he was of Amy, Sophie, and Becca. But why had he felt it necessary to emphasize that Dean was Hayley's boyfriend? Buddy hadn't even called Dean her ex.

"We're working on it," Dorn said.

"When?" Buddy stepped closer, getting in Dorn's face. Well, as much as he could, being a foot shorter than the seven-plus-foot tall alien. It was surreal seeing someone towering over her brother. "I guess you guys have already hooked up with my sisters, so you can cross that off your list of things to-do before finding Hayley."

Dorn's spine plates rose, a warning vibration

reverberating throughout the room. "Your sisters are our soulmates. Bonding with them is the sacred will of our goddess."

"Yeah?" Buddy pointed at Amy. "The same goddess that altered their bodies without asking? What about *their* will in all this? Did they ask to be your soulmates?"

"Buddy," Dorn began.

Amy grabbed Buddy by his shoulder and spun him around to face her. Too bad she used her left arm and momentarily forgot about its augmentation. Buddy flew back again, this time, landing hard on his back and skidding across the floor. When he stopped, he shook his head, dazed. He rolled to his side, pushing himself to all fours. Amy rushed to help him up.

"I'm so sorry," she said. "I'm still getting used to my strength."

"You shouldn't have to be." His gray eyes glittered in the light, reflecting the silver of his uniform. Amy's stomach twisted, the hairs on her arm rising as an odd tremor swept over her skin.

"This is all their fault," Buddy said. "They pulled you into this, and now some superpowered alien has altered you, just like she altered Sophie. We have no idea what it's going to do to you."

A superpowered alien? That made more sense than a goddess. Maybe.

Amy knew she was different, but she just assumed it

was from the technology the Cygnians had used to heal her. This was the first she was hearing about being altered purposefully. She would definitely have words with Dorn on that later.

"Our goddess seeks only what is best for our people," Dorn said.

"*Your* people," Buddy spat. "My sisters are Earthlings."

"With the souls of Cygnian warriors, making them part of our people." Dorn shook his head, his sadness rolling toward her. "I thought you would understand. You've spent so much time with us. You are an honorary member of our prism."

"Yeah, I understood all right," Buddy said. "Up until you started pairing off with my sisters."

"Stop," Amy yelled. What the hell was up with Buddy? He had seemed upset when Kral crashed their family dinner, but this was absolutely next level.

"None of this is helping us get Hayley back," Amy said.

"What do you suggest we do?" Dorn shifted his weight, his stance ready. He was actually looking to her for guidance. It was so strange to have someone take her seriously.

"Just let me think," she said.

She went back over everything she knew about Dean, which wasn't much. Sophie hadn't spoken to Amy about Hayley's boyfriend, but Amy was good at ferreting out secrets. Baby sisters were talented that way, especially ones who needed to work on their stealth observation skills for their chosen career path.

From the side of the conversation that Amy could hear through the vent separating her room from Sophie's, Hayley and Dean had met in Paris. Dean was rich, hot, and mysterious. Sophie had pushed hard for the pair to get together, but Hayley had misgivings about the relationship. Sophie goaded her into ignoring her instincts. Hayley sensed something was off.

Amy sensed it, too. And she wasn't about to ignore her instincts.

Something in Amy shifted. Dorn felt her emotions change, a subtle thread of purpose weaving in among the anger, fear, and determination that had flooded her when she learned of Hayley's abduction. Her mood tensed, though her stance dropped into the easy readiness he had seen in her before their combat earlier.

She circled around Buddy, standing on his opposite side so that her brother was flanked by herself and Dorn, but not so directly that they would be in each other's crossfire. Her focus was intent upon Buddy. She was targeting him as if he was a threat.

Dorn scrutinized Buddy, trying to pick up on whatever

Amy was detecting. He could see nothing suspicious about his friend. Buddy didn't lose his temper often with the Cygnians in Dorn's prism, but it had happened before and it almost always involved his family or sisters. Dorn hadn't thought it out of character, but Amy knew her brother better.

Did she think he might actually be Dean? No, it was impossible for him to sneak onto the station. *Outreach* had scanners that would detect Scorpiians. At least, they thought they would. Feeling Amy's continued unease, Dorn began to wonder.

"If only Hayley had broken up with Dean sooner," Amy said, angling her head so it looked like she wasn't paying much attention to Buddy, though she kept him in her periphery. "She wasn't interested in him from the start."

Buddy's brow furrowed. "What do you mean? Sophie says they were crazy about each other."

Amy snorted. "Sophie just wanted to finally be able to go on double-dates. Hayley's standards were so high, no one could meet them."

"Yeah, well… Apparently this Dean guy did," Buddy said.

"She only dated him because Sophie goaded her into it," Amy said.

Buddy took a menacing step forward. "That's not true."

"My room is right next to Sophie's," she said. "I could

hear their conversations through the vent."

Buddy glowered at her, his hands still curled into fists. Amy smirked, a rush of victory flooding through her.

"So, you're pissed as hell that we're hooking up with your close friends, but it's okay for Hayley to have the hots for an alien dickweed?" Amy made a tutting noise. "Gosh, Buddy. That seems out of character."

The tension drained out of Buddy's body, his shoulders dropping and an odd smile crossing his face. As he relaxed, the opposite happened to Dorn. His stomach felt as though it was turning to ice, his hearts beat more rapidly, urging Amy's to speed up. His skin felt electrified, ready to face battle with his mate. Buddy waved a finger at Amy, his posture and gestures, even his expression, was so unlike anything Dorn had seen before from his friend.

Buddy shook his head, and said, "That wasn't very nice of you. Toying with my emotions."

Amy shrugged. "On Earth, we call that 'getting a taste of your own medicine.'"

"I knew you would be a problem." He let out a small laugh, his skin rippling and glowing with a bright silver light. The silver of his uniform melted into his body, changing shape along with the rest of him. When the light faded, a tall, thin man stood before them, dressed in a formal Earth suit. His eyes were dark brown, as was his hair, which stood up in an odd tousled style.

"But, since you're the only sister available, I'm going

to have to make do." Dean strolled closer to the regen bed, one hand in his pocket and the other at his side, his posture casual and relaxed. The shapeshifter knew he had the upper hand. Dorn agreed. There was no way he and Amy could take on a Scorpiian and win. But from the confidence and assessment flowing from Amy, she had no idea.

Her strategy of flanking her target would have been fine if Dean were an Earthling or even a Cygnian, but he was an altogether different lifeform. Dorn tried to project a sense of warning to her, but she only glanced at him, scowling. How could Dorn protect her? Even with her heightened abilities and the Cygnian wristbands, she was still human. Dorn was nearly indestructible, giving him a better chance of surviving the encounter. Amy wasn't.

"I'm on a tight schedule, so I'm going to be straight with you," Dean said.

Amy snorted as if she found it hard to believe in his honesty. Dorn was right there with her. Dean just smirked.

"Amy is going to come with me," Dean said. "I won't harm her and will return her to you as soon as your prism returns what they took from me."

"I'm not going anywhere with you," Amy said. "And if Dorn's friends took something from you, I'm sure they had a good reason."

"I don't give a shit about their reason." Dean's voice actually rose in pitch, his lip curling up in anger briefly.

"They have what's mine, and I want it back."

What was he talking about? Dorn scoured his memories, trying to think of something they might have obtained that belonged to the Scorpiian, but nothing came to him.

"We don't have anything that belongs to you." Dorn took a step closer to Amy, desperate to get her out of this situation.

"And as I said, I'm not going anywhere," Amy said.

Dean smiled at Dorn. "It's cute that she thinks she has a choice in this."

She lifted her arms, tapping on the controls of her wristband that brought up her shields, her fingers hovering over the blaster panel. Dorn sent her his desperate need for her to wait. He knew there was little chance of them doing permanent harm to Dean. He would use his shapeshifting abilities to heal any wounds they inflicted on him. And in the frenzy of battle, she could get hurt. Dorn had to find a way to engage Dean himself, to get Amy to safety, but he doubted she would leave his side.

"When I heard about the… *augmentations* you and your sisters received, it inspired me to do some more upgrades as well," Dean said. "Especially with what I've learned about you, Dorn."

What was he talking about? How could a Scorpiian 'upgrade' themself? Icy dread clenched Dorn's stomach.

"There's something I want to show you," Dean said. A

little trip down memory lane." He flashed a smile as his skin began to glow with an intense silver light.

Chapter Fourteen

"Amy, look out!" Dorn shouted, reaching for her.

Amy ducked underneath a gleaming line of silver, curling her body into a ball and rolling, then springing back to her feet on the other side of Dean. At least she was closer to the door. Dorn was trapped with the still-shifting Scorpiian—nothing but the transparent material of the viewport behind him.

He remembered how Amy had tried to space him and activated his atmospheric shielding, just in case her earlier plan once more became a viable strategy. He didn't know how he was going to fight this… whatever it was. What the hell was Dean turning into that was so huge? Dorn didn't think Scorpiians could shift so much of their mass.

A rumbling vibration resonated in Dorn's chest, jarring his hearts. The sound coalesced into a voice just as Dean's body settled into its new form, so huge, it took up a third of the room.

Dorn couldn't breathe. His hearts pounded so fiercely, his battered lungs struggled to bring in air. His eyes were wide, his skin prickling as if he was standing next to an unshielded plasma core. It couldn't be this. It couldn't be.

Not with Amy so close. So vulnerable.

"What do you think?" Dean asked, the depth of his voice making Dorn's teeth vibrate. "I chose this form just for you. Well, maybe not *just* for you. I think Bron would find it nostalgic as well, wouldn't he?"

How did Dean know about Bron? About what had happened so long ago on Cygnus-Prime? The creature in front of him shouldn't have been able to speak. Dean must have modified its vocal chords. It took a step closer, one massive hoof gouging a furrow in the metal floor as it snorted a challenge. Its gleaming blue flank caught and reflected the lights, rippling over contours of sinew and muscle. Long antlers scraped the ceiling of the room, showering sparks down on them. Its demonic eyes glowed with a fiery red light.

"Run…" Dorn barely had air to form the word. He sucked in a deep breath, expanding his lungs, then shouted, "Amy, run!"

"What?" she yelled. "I'm not leaving you."

The beryl beast kicked out with its back leg, easily tearing the regen bed from its mountings on the floor. It flew across the room, landing in front of the exit.

"Stay," the beast said. "See how brave your warrior mate can be when facing his worst nightmare."

Dorn had never seen such an enormous beryl beast. They couldn't even space it by breaking the viewport. It wouldn't fit through the framework. Dorn and Amy would be blown to safety at least, if they had to resort to that. The regen bed blocked most of the door, but there was a small gap along one side. Amy might be able to push it aside with her enhanced strength if Dorn could distract the beast.

"How about I kick your ass and spare us all the time?" Amy lifted her wristbands, her finger drawing along the blaster control.

"Don't," Dorn yelled, but he was too late.

The blast hit the beryl's pelt, glancing off harmlessly, but ricocheting back at her. Amy yelped and leapt to the side. She tapped a few more controls, her shields glowing brighter.

"Okay," she said. "New strategy."

"I'm more interested in the old," the beryl said. It swung its head toward Amy, scoring deep grooves in the ceiling as it did. More sparks rained down on her, fizzing as they hit her personal shielding. "Tell me, Dorn, did the beryl take your brother's leg with its antlers or its hooves? Maybe its teeth?" The beryl gnashed its teeth together with a menacing clack. "I'm thinking hooves with how much of his torso and chest needed to be replaced with machinery as well. I want to be accurate as Amy and I recreate the scene for you."

Dorn's body burned as if it had been filled with acid. His muscles were desperate to move, but he was frozen in place. Anything he did would put Amy in more danger. She was worried, but not afraid, her confidence in herself

—in him—bolstering her even in the face of this monster. Dorn was utterly terrified. He didn't try to shield her from the emotion. He knew what a normal beryl could do, and this thing was even worse.

His mind filled with images of Bron as a child lying in a field, the beryl on top of him, pawing his body into ribbons as the hunting party tried to pull it away. Dorn had told their father that Bron was too young to hunt a beryl. His skin and muscle hadn't finished hardening as adult Cygnians' did, giving them their near-invulnerability. Their father hadn't listened.

"How long till station security arrives?" Amy said. When Dorn didn't reply, she raised her voice. "Dorn! How long do we have to hold this thing off?"

His hearts sank. "They aren't coming. I told them we'd be… occupied. And that there might be unusual sensor readings from the room."

"Well, shit." Amy inched along the wall as the beryl followed with its gaze, a low chuckle rumbling out from it.

"What's its weak spot?" she said. "Dorn?"

"There is no weak spot." His voice was tight and harsh. Why wouldn't she listen to him and run?

A dozen Cygnian warriors had trouble taking down a beryl beast on their homeworld, and that was with the heightened gravity slowing it down. They had specialized weapons for hunting beryls, pulse blasters that could disrupt its nervous system and yl-etok for gripping its neck and breaking it—which required every warrior using all of their strength.

"Just tell me what you want," Dorn yelled. "I'll find it. I'll get it for you."

Shock and disbelief flowed through his bond with Amy. Her anger followed, though it was tempered. Probably from sensing the fear and shame Dorn was drowning in. He hadn't been able to protect his brother so many years ago. He didn't know how to protect Amy now. But he couldn't just stand there and do nothing.

"I don't know why this giant antelope… bison… whatever is freaking you out, but snap out of it," she said. "It's just Dean messing with you."

A rumbling laugh came from the beryl's chest. "You really should have talked more before getting married. You ended up with the only Cygnian warrior I've ever heard of who's loaded down with emotional baggage. At least you're not bonded to his brother. Well, what's left of him."

Rage blasted through Dorn, stronger than his fear. He roared as he threw himself forward, locking his arms around the beryl's neck. He knew he wasn't strong enough to kill it, but that wouldn't stop him from trying. At the very least, he could pull its attention away from Amy long enough for her to get help.

But it wasn't a beryl he was fighting. Not really.

Sinuous silver tendrils lifted from its back, wrapping around Dorn's arms and chest and squeezing tight. He gasped as his breath was forced out of him.

Scorpiians couldn't do this. When they were in an assumed form, they were stuck in it. That was the only thing that stopped them from being the most dangerous entities in the galaxy. They were close enough already. And the strength in this body—Dean's ability to replicate not just form, but the abilities of the creature, to enhance them even…

What the hell were they facing?

Amy shouted as she saw the tendrils crushing Dorn to the beryl's body. She leapt up, grabbing onto one of its antlers and using her position to kick the side of its face. Dean had managed to replicate the beryl's invulnerable hide. Her feet didn't faze him a bit. Dorn sensed another purpose, a plan brewing inside of her. The emotion reminded him too much of their challenge, when she had been about to try to space him. She needed to run, not fight, but Dorn couldn't draw enough breath to speak. His lungs burned, his chest aching from the pressure as Dean squeezed harder.

Amy swung her legs around, gripping the beryl's snout between her knees. Dorn felt a slight vibration ripple through the beast. It was laughing.

"That's very inappropriate," Dean said, his rough voice booming in the room. "You're a married woman, and I'm spoken for."

Dorn couldn't get enough leverage to loosen Dean's

hold on him, couldn't break free of the Scorpiian's grip. Amy managed to grab the antler closer to Dorn with her right arm. Was she trying to get to him? To see if she could free Dorn from Dean's grasp? Dorn tried to will her away, projecting his desire for her to be safe, but knew she wouldn't listen.

"Hayley would never fall for a shit like you," Amy said. "She's too smart for that, and she's way too good for you."

Dean's grip tightened. The edges of Dorn's vision faded to black.

"We'll see about that when we find her," Dean said.

A burst of surprise and confusion hit Dorn, blasting out from Amy. Her focus and determination quickly returned.

"I don't think you'll be seeing much of anything," Amy said.

She pulled back her left arm and plunged her fist into Dean's eye, all the way up to her shoulder. Dean let out a horrible bellow, rearing back and puncturing the ceiling above them. The tendrils holding Dorn loosened. He planted his feet against the beryl's side and pushed away, breaking Dean's hold, then flipped in mid-air so that he landed on his feet in a crouch. The moment his feet hit the ground, he leapt up, aiming for his soulmate, desperate to get her away from this thing.

She jerked her arm back, silver fluid spraying the ceiling. As Dorn's arms connected with her torso, she released her grip on the beryl, her movements in perfect synchronicity with Dorn's. Dorn spun her around and tucked her against his chest, landing with her held tightly in his arms. The beryl staggered back a few paces, shaking its head. It quickly calmed, breathing heavily, then began to laugh again.

The silver on the ceiling and coating Amy's arm dropped to the floor, flowing in rivulets towards Dean. When it touched his body, it merged with him. He shook his head again, the eye Amy had gouged glowing silver. He blinked a few times, then opened it wide. It was as if nothing had happened.

Dorn felt Amy's disappointment, reflecting his own. How could they possibly face off against this?

The door to the room slid open, a grating, metallic sound matching the movement as it became stuck halfway. Perhaps station security had come to assist after all. Dorn would take any help they could get, but he didn't see anyone in the hallway beyond. At first, he thought it was a mechanical malfunction, but then he heard a small voice from the narrow gap at the side of the regen bed.

"Okay, that will be fun to climb on later." Queenie ran into the room, her neck crooked so she could keep looking at the regen bed. "I came to check on Amy and—"

Queenie turned to face the room and the kitten's eyes grew so wide, Dorn could see the whites around them. Her pupils dilated, her fur was sticking straight out over her entire body making her look twice as big. She turned sideways, back arched, tail stiff, ears flat against her head, and let out a long hiss.

"Queenie, get out of here." Amy shifted to stand between the kitten and the beryl. The huge beast took one step back, then another.

"What is that *thing*?" Queenie cried.

Dean jerked his head back, but instead of attacking, silver light coated his body. As the light shrank into a more humanoid silhouette, he leapt to the ceiling, his new shape still coalescing. His torso elongated, with multiple pairs of arms extending from his sides. His head broadened into a triangular shape with two antennae protruding from it. The glow faded, revealing an Antarean.

"Holy crap, a giant ant person." Amy ducked down to grab Queenie, crouching low as Dean scurried over the ceiling above them.

"Wait." Queenie scrabbled frantically against Amy's hold.

"Sweetie, stop," Amy said. "I'm going to drop you if you keep that up."

"I *want* you to drop me," Queenie spat. "Let me go." She turned her gaze to Dean as she yelled, "I need to talk to you. Dean!"

The shifted Scorpiian paused at the top of the regen bed, his narrow body pressed into the space between the bed and the ceiling. Queenie stilled in Amy's arms.

"I'm sorry," Queenie said. "Please, don't go."

He turned back to them, his huge insectoid eyes strobing a dull indigo. Then he turned back to the door and disappeared through the gap.

Chapter Fifteen

Amy's chest hurt from the way her heart pounded and her lungs took in quick breaths. The terror of facing down that creature finally began to register now that it wasn't in the room with her. Her body shook as the adrenaline flooding her system started to subside. The soft kitten in her arms should have been reassuring, but Queenie had started clawing at Amy's hands again. Amy was going to need more time in the regen bed at this point.

She glanced at the bed blocking the door. Well, a different regen bed. Queenie finally stopped struggling, but then lashed out, biting Amy's thumb hard enough to draw blood.

"Ow," Amy yelled. "Queenie, what are you doing?"

"What are *you* doing, human?" Queenie yelled. "Why didn't you let me go to him? He's my friend."

Amy couldn't believe it. "That *thing*?"

"Don't you dare call him that," Queenie said, her voice fierce. "He hates it when people call him that." As she continued, a plaintive note filled her words. "And *I* called him a thing. He must be so hurt." She turned her face up to Amy, tears welling in the corners of her golden eyes. "He heard me say I was sorry. Why didn't he stay?"

"Sweetie..." Amy's voice trailed off. She didn't know how to respond, what to think.

So much more was going on here than she had even realized. Queenie considered Dean a friend. From the way he stopped mid-fight when he was obliterating them, Amy had to wonder if there wasn't something between the pair. She would have to get to the bottom of that, but more importantly, Dean had let something huge slip during their battle. Something that left her suspended between a glimmer of hope and an even deeper despair than she had felt earlier.

"He doesn't have her," Amy said. "Dean doesn't have Hayley."

Dorn approached them, wrapping his arms around Amy and pulling her close, though he left enough space for the little kitten. "You picked up on that, too?"

Amy pulled back enough to grimace at him. She let her emotions express her displeasure at him doubting her. Her anger quickly turned to worry.

"The only lead we had was Dean," Amy said. "If he doesn't have Hayley, how do we have any chance of finding her?"

"I can ask him," Queenie said. "If he'll just talk to me."

Amy lifted the little kitten so that she could look into Queenie's eyes. She thought through how to broach the subject, not wanting to alienate the calico. Straight-on didn't seem the best approach, so she decided on a different tack.

"How did you and Dean meet?" Amy asked.

"I'm not…" Queenie bowed her head. "I'm not supposed to say."

Amy's anger toward Dean grew. That was a classic manipulative tactic. Isolate your asset to keep them dependent on you, to keep them loyal.

"I get that you want to help your friend, but people are in danger," Amy said, making her voice as gentle as she could. Queenie turned her face away and let out a little snort of breath. "Queenie, please. I'm your friend, too, aren't I?" Amy hated herself for using that tactic as well, but at the same time, she needed to help Queenie—and to figure out the dynamic between the kitten and Dean. Besides, Amy meant it. She did think of the kitten as a friend.

Queenie trembled in Amy's hands, leaning closer to her palms. Amy held her against her chest, petting her forehead with one finger.

"I'm sorry to upset you," Amy said. "I just don't want anyone to get hurt."

"Was that really him?" Queenie's voice was so small. "Was that Dean?"

"It was." Dorn's voice was gentler then Amy had ever heard it. He still had his arms around them protectively.

"They told me he was bad," Queenie said. "My brother

and sister. But I didn't believe them. Dean was always so nice to me. Even before he knew I was smart. Before I could talk."

Amy's brow furrowed. "You haven't always been able to talk?"

"No." Queenie shook her little head. "A Vegan engineer named Peri made us these collars that let you understand us. We could always understand you."

There were implications to that. Helpful implications. If Dean had spent time with Queenie before he knew she was smart, before she could talk, he might have given away secrets that could help them against him. Secrets that could help find Hayley. The flip side of it was, if he had hung out with Queenie before he knew she could be of any use to him, he might actually like the kitten instead of seeing her as an asset to be used for his gain.

Nobody was all good or all bad. Amy shook away the doubts, focusing on the cold reality of their situation. Hayley was missing, and Dean was their best chance of learning anything that might help them find her. In fact, he seemed eager to find her as well.

"Does Dean have enemies?" Amy asked, a thought forming in her mind.

Dorn glared at her, anger flowing from him in harsh waves. "He's a Scorpiian. They're universally reviled—and for good reason."

Amy remembered what Dean had said. How he had

used the form of that creature to mess with Dorn's head as much as his body—maybe more. She would have to ask about what had happened with his brother as soon as she could. Queenie let out an indignant snort, narrowing her eyes as she stared at Dorn from the corner of her eyes.

"Spoken like an arrogant Cygnian," Queenie said.

"Arrogant?" Dorn's eyebrows rose. "I'm guessing you heard that from your shapeshifting friend."

She sniffed dismissively. "Perhaps."

"I'm trying to get at something here," Amy said. "And you two picking at each other isn't helping. I mean a specific enemy. Someone recent and with a grudge."

"I don't understand," Dorn said.

"Dean wants to find Hayley, too," Amy said. "He's going to pretty big lengths to do so. Whoever took her managed to get her from a Scorpiian, and I have to admit, after facing him down, I see what the big deal is."

"Dean is unlike any Scorpiian I've ever heard of," Dorn said. "His abilities are much stronger."

"Dean is the most powerful Scorpiian that has ever existed." Queenie puffed herself up, a note of pride ringing in her voice. "He goes beyond learning new skills. He's utterly committed to becoming the best specimen he can be."

"Specimen?" Amy said. "Does he talk about himself that way? Like he's some… science experiment?"

Queenie's eyes widened, and she tucked her nose close

against Amy's chest. Another piece to the puzzle. If Dean saw himself as an experiment, who was the scientist pulling the strings? Amy glanced over at Dorn and saw the same concerns mirrored in his eyes. She was about to ask, to make sure her assumptions were accurate and they were on the same page, when a sibilant voice came over some unseen speakers in the room.

"Amy Myers, your presence is required at Station Command."

"Shit," she said. "What was that?"

"The Vegan Station Commander." Queenie ducked her head again. "It means you're in trouble."

Walking toward the command ops should have been an amazing experience. Now that she wasn't running, Amy could actually take in her surroundings. The corridors near the medical bays were all made of that white material with black panels, but they also had pretty lights running along them. The corridors opened up into what must be the central core, the ceiling suddenly several stories above her, with lush plants growing along the walls.

She saw what she first thought were birds flying above them, but then realized they were more of the giant ant people that Dean had turned into. She pressed herself closer to Dorn. Any one of those could be the Scorpiian.

Dorn had already alerted station command to Dean's presence and last known form before they left the med bay, but they were all doubtful their scans would reveal the Scorpiian's location.

Amy's heart beat faster the closer they came to their destination, mentally listing her transgressions as they approached. Assaulting station personnel. Trespassing in restricted areas maybe? Hell, she had tried to blast a hole in the space station's exterior. To her, the act had made sense at the time. To Station Command… Yeah, they were probably going to frown upon that.

Dorn paused before a large set of gunmetal gray double doors. He reached down and interlaced their fingers. Her other hand was still clutching Queenie against her chest. With a brief nod, Amy let him know she was ready. There was no sense putting this off. Dorn turned back to the door and pressed his hand against a small panel next to it. After a moment, the door slid open. Worried as she was, Amy still was overcome with wonder as she stepped into the space station's command hub.

Consoles protruded from the walls, their ergonomic shapes and the odd stick-shaped 'chairs' in front of them not making sense at first until Amy saw the aliens perching on them—the biggest iguanas she had ever seen. Or maybe they looked more like basilisk lizards. It was hard to say, aside from calling them lizard people. These must be the Vegans.

They lounged on the stick-chairs, much like a normal reptile, but their arms stretched forward to work the controls before them. Each emerald-green lizard had black stripes crossing their backs, extending from their spines. The stripes were outlined with different colors. On top of that, they wore metallic bands that gleamed silver in the light reflecting off the white walls. The bands encircled their neck, arms, legs, and even their tails, with more of the metal covering their backs and partly protecting their rib cages.

One of the Vegans stood in front of them, hands clasped behind its back and tail whipping back and forth as it stared at a blank wall. The Vegan turned as they entered. Amy's heart was in her throat. She refused to let herself lean closer to Dorn, though she wanted to. The Vegan was only three and a half feet tall, standing on its back legs. Its eyes were large and golden, with narrow slits for pupils. Its face was flatter than a lizard's, giving it a more human-like appearance. The scales of its stomach were a paler green then the rest of it.

"Greetings," it said, drawing out the 'S.' It bowed low. "I am Cerulean."

Queenie piped up with, "He's in charge of all the Vegans on the station."

Cerulean arched an eyebrow ridge as he stared at the kitten. "I see that you have met our resident volunteer security infiltrator."

Queenie snorted, then said, "That's his way of saying I get into things I shouldn't."

"Quite successfully at that." Cerulean shocked Amy with a smile.

Dorn reached down to pet the kitten, and said, "Is that so? I might have a position for you on the *Arrow*. I could use an assistant."

Amy's heart lurched at the thought. She had always wanted a cat, but being in a family full of dog people, it had never happened. The closest she came was the family's Pomeranians, which… really wasn't the same at all. The idea of having Queenie with her while she was with Dorn was a welcome distraction from her situation.

It didn't last long.

"We have received a message for you." Cerulean straightened, his demeanor turning somber. He stepped back and gestured toward the front wall of the ops center.

The entire wall flickered with light, coalescing in a view of Dean's face. Amy did step closer to Dorn then. She wished the image was smaller. At the same time, the size gave her a chance to scrutinize his surroundings. She could see white walls with black panels over his shoulder. He was still on the station. At least, he had been when he made this recording. Unfortunately, there were no other identifying characteristics of his location and he had zoomed in on his face, covering most of the area behind him. All the walls looked the same in this place.

"Hello, Amy." Dean's smooth voice rolled over them as the recording began to play. He was back in his human form, brown eyes flashing on the screen. His suit had been replaced with a black turtleneck sweater. "I'm not going to bother with posturing or threats. I understand you well enough to know that's a waste of time for both of us. What I will tell you about is this. My contingency plan. If you're seeing this recording, it's in effect."

He must have prepared this in advance, just in case he wasn't able to get her where he wanted her. But where was that? And what did he hope to achieve?

"One of them, anyway," he continued. "Let's hope we don't have to go too far down the list. They get messier as they go."

Her stomach clenched at the thought. Things had already gotten messy back in the med bay. What exactly was he alluding to?

"The Cygnians have my lockbox," Dean said. "I want it back."

"The lockbox is *his*?" Dorn murmured. "We thought it belonged to Norem."

She was vaguely reassured that Dorn knew what Dean was talking about. It also didn't last long.

"The original plan—" Dean angled his head and looked up for a moment. "Well, the *current* plan, I should say—was to trade you to the Cygnians for the lockbox. The *original* plan involved killing Becca. And you, I guess. Or

Sophie." He waved his hand dismissively. "Either one would have been fine."

Amy sucked in a breath, her skin prickling with adrenaline. She felt Queenie begin to tremble in her hands and held the kitten more snugly to her chest.

"Now…" He laughed casually, as if he hadn't just been talking about hurting her family. About *killing* them. "I just really want my lockbox back. So, I propose a different trade."

Amy's heart stuttered in her chest. What could Dean have that he thought was valuable enough to get the lockbox from them? Dean leaned closer to the camera, leaving a pause between each word in which Amy's heartbeat almost deafened her.

"I… have… Buddy," he said.

Chapter Sixteen

Queenie let out a mournful yowl. "He *is* bad. How could I have been so wrong about him?"

Amy snuggled her closer, letting go of Dorn's hand, even though her mind and heart were reeling so much that the room seemed to spin. Queenie nuzzled Amy's face, then gently pawed her cheek.

"I'm so sorry," Queenie said.

"He might not…" Amy's voice had a rasp, the words crackling and raw. "He might be lying. He might not have Buddy."

Queenie winced, then shook her head. A low meow accompanied her words. "He does. If he says he does, he does. Dean takes the people he's duplicating and keeps them in stasis in his chamber."

Amy's heart felt like it was shattering. Her stomach must be full of thumbtacks from how it hurt and her voice was rough when she spoke again.

"We can't negotiate with him," she said. "We can't give him what he wants."

If Dean wanted the lockbox that badly, Amy couldn't imagine what he would use it for. They couldn't give him something that might make him even more powerful.

Dorn put his arm around her shoulders, pulling her close. He rested his other hand on Queenie's head.

"How do you know about Dean's methods?" he asked the kitten.

"He talked about it when we spent time together on the *Reckoning*," Queenie said.

"Wait, you were with him on the *Reckoning*?" Amy asked, a glimmer of hope flickering to life within her, making her heart race. She felt the response to her excitement in Dorn as his own hearts matched her beat. "That ship protecting Earth and our solar system?"

"Yes, we always met there," Queenie said.

"When you say his chamber, do you mean it was on that ship as well?" Amy's voice rose in pitch along with her excitement. "On the *Reckoning*?"

"Yes…" Queenie cocked her head to the side.

"Do you know what that means?" Amy looked up at Dorn.

He nodded. "That we can find Buddy and rescue him."

"Do you have schematics for the *Reckoning*?" Amy asked, turning to Cerulean.

Already, his mate was strategizing, coming up with alternate scenarios. Dorn had some of his own. Plans that

Amy would not necessarily agree with.

"We do, however, the chamber you are looking for does not appear on it," the Vegan said.

"That's fine." Amy waved her hand dismissively. "Can you scan the ship? Like thoroughly?"

"Yes." Cerulean dragged out the word as if he was skeptical about whatever she had in mind.

Amy nodded, her excitement rising. "We can analyze the dead space. See if any rooms scan at different dimensions than the schematic lists."

"That is… very clever," Cerulean said.

He turned to the Vegan at his side, a smaller female with deep red contours outlining the black stripes, and hissed a series of commands in their sibilant tongue. The center of the room filled with a floating holoprojection of the *Reckoning*—the image made of blue, transparent light instead of a true-to-life depiction. Amy's eyes widened, but then she stepped closer, scrutinizing the ship.

"It's enormous," she said.

"The *Reckoning* is one of two remaining Coalition warships," Cerulean said. "It houses a large number of their soldiers and functions as a mobile colony vessel, as well as providing additional protection to the Sol system."

"So, there are plenty of people for Dean to replicate." Amy chewed on her lip as she stared at the vessel, a stronger focus and determination emanating from her than Dorn had ever felt. He wondered how it would be affected by what he was about to tell her.

"I'm heading to the *Reckoning* now," Dorn said.

That got Amy's attention. She wheeled around, concern etched on her features and transferring to him through their bond.

"Why?" she asked.

"You already know." He gripped her waist and pulled her close.

Queenie started to squirm in Amy's grasp. "Let me down. You two are about to get all kissy-face again, and I don't want to get squished."

Amy laughed, then bent to release the kitten. Queenie ran to a corner and started licking her paw. Amy turned back to Dorn, and he pulled her close again. He let his love for her fill his hearts and flow to her, trying to send her a reassurance he was still convincing himself of.

"We need to be able to act the moment we find Buddy," Dorn said. "If I'm on board the ship, we're that much closer."

She looked aside, her emotions fighting a battle within her. For once, fear seemed to be dominating.

"Tell me," he said.

"What we fought, that creature…" She shook her head, then looked back to the wall that had shown the recording of Dean. "But we don't want to tip Dean off that we're onto him."

"And that's why you're staying here."

Dorn felt her frustration mount. She knew he was right, had already planned to stay. Knowing didn't make it any easier for her to stay behind. It would be the same for him if their roles were reversed.

"If Dean reaches out again, you need to be here," Dorn said. "He's focused on you, not me."

"Great," she said. "I'm the diversion."

"A vital aspect of most infiltration plans," he said.

She frowned at him, but then stepped closer. Wrapping her arms around his neck, she pulled him down for a deep, lingering kiss. Dorn gripped her waist, closing the space between them. The kiss intensified, electric arcs of pleasure sweeping over his skin, his spine plates vibrating with need.

"Ahem." Cerulean cleared his throat behind them.

Dorn looked over to see the Vegan staring intently at the holodisplay, his cheeks flushed with a tinge of pink. Amy smirked and stepped back from Dorn, but left her hand on his chest.

"Come back to me in one piece, okay?" she said.

He smiled, loving the concern he felt through their bond, though she betrayed so little of it with her expression. His mate was perfect for him in so many ways.

"I intend to," he said, then turned and strode from the room. The sooner he found Buddy, the better.

Dorn headed for the hangar bays, eager to get to his shard. Before he did, there was someone he needed to contact. He had a plan to rescue Buddy, but he wouldn't rely on it being successful. Dean wasn't the only one who made contingency plans. Ducking into a storage room, Dorn activated the communication function of his wristband, keying in Bron's channel. It didn't take long for his brother to respond.

"What?" Bron's taciturn greeting was nothing new. Dorn's hearts beat more strongly, his mouth going dry as he tried to think of what to say to bridge the gap between them. He reined in his emotions, not wanting Amy to pick up on them. Enough time passed that Bron spoke again, a hint of concern edging into his tone. "Dorn?"

"I'm here," Dorn managed. "I need your help."

"I'll get the others," Bron said.

"No, *your* help. Please."

Bron's voice became guarded. "Is something wrong?"

What *wasn't* wrong? Okay, that wasn't fair. Everything about Amy was right. Their union, their bond. But it was surrounded by such dangerous circumstances.

"I'm not sure how much I can share safely, so I'm asking you to trust me," Dorn said.

"Always."

The sincerity in Bron's tone, the lack of hesitation, tightened Dorn's throat with emotion. Even with everything they had been through, Bron still trusted Dorn. Dorn wanted to believe it wasn't just that they were prism mates, but that it went beyond that. That it was because they were brothers.

"I need the lockbox here," Dorn said. "Tell the others… I don't know, tell them whatever you need to get it here without raising their alarm."

"The very fact that you're asking this of me is causing me my own alarm."

"Please, trust me. I wouldn't be asking if it wasn't important. You can't even tell Amy."

There was a long pause before Bron said, "Keeping secrets from your mate is not a good way to begin a relationship."

"I know."

Dorn didn't plan to give the lockbox to Dean. Having it close was merely a safety measure. If things didn't go as they hoped, having the lockbox could provide them with leverage they might desperately need.

"I'll be there as soon as I can," Bron said.

Dorn's chest relaxed, his hearts slowing a bit and filling with gratitude. Before Bron could end the transmission, Dorn said, "Brother…"

The pause was even longer than the last. Bron's voice was utterly shielded when he replied with a cautious, "Yes?"

"When you arrive… I'd like to talk. Really talk."

After a moment, Bron said, “I suppose it’s time we did.”

Dorn let out a breath and nodded, though his brother couldn’t see the gesture.

“Watch your back,” Dorn said.

“I always do.” There was a hint of a smile in Bron’s voice. The transmission ended.

Dorn didn’t have the luxury of taking a moment to collect himself. He strode back into the corridor, his long strides eating up the distance between himself and the hangars. As he turned the last corner before his bay, Queenie appeared at the end of the hall, scampering toward him.

“Thank goodness,” she said, her voice a bit breathless. “I thought I’d missed you.”

“What do you need, little one?”

She snorted, eyes narrowing at him, but didn’t slow her pace. Her paws hit his boots and she leapt up, claws digging into his tunic as she climbed all the way to his shoulder. She leaned closer, rubbing her face against his cheek. Her fur was one of the softest things he’d ever felt.

“I need to come with you, of course,” she said.

Dorn’s eyes widened. There was no way he was taking a child with him on his mission.

“Absolutely not.” He reached up to pluck her from his shoulder, but she dug her claws deeper into the leather of his tunic. The hide rose with her. If he used more force to try to dislodge her, he might hurt the kitten, so he set her back down.

"It's too dangerous for you to come," he said.

She snorted again, the sound accompanied by something akin to a sneeze. "It's too dangerous for *you* to try to leave me behind. I know Dean. How he operates. Plus, I can take you to his chamber."

That was hard to resist.

"Can't you just tell me where it is?" he asked.

"No." She shook her head, a quick meow emphasizing her collar's translation.

"Go back to Station Command and talk Amy through it. She has schematics for the *Reckoning* you can use to pinpoint the location."

"I can't describe it. I can only take you there."

"Queenie—" he began, but she cut him off.

"How is it any safer here than on the *Reckoning*?" she said. "Dean could be anywhere. Or anyone. In fact, since we know he's on *Outreach* station, the *Reckoning* is probably a safer place to be. At least, we know he *isn't* there."

Her logic was sound, though at this point, Dean would already have had enough time to get back to the warship. Queenie was right. He could be anywhere or anyone. The thought wasn't comforting. Nowhere was safe.

"We're wasting time," Queenie said. "Come on."

Dorn shook his head, but headed into the hangar bay.

His single-person fighter was hovering a few feet off the ground inside the chamber, the milky white crystal of the ship reflecting the lights in the bay and projecting rainbow patterns on the dark gray walls.

Queenie sucked in a breath. "I have to admit, your ships are certainly the prettiest I've ever seen."

"And the most indestructible," Dorn said with a smirk. It wasn't just Cygnian warriors that were hard to destroy. Everything on their planet had to be extremely resilient to survive the intense gravity and radiation of the nearby black hole.

The shard's hatch opened as he approached and he climbed aboard, lying on his stomach in front of the controls. Queenie crawled onto his back as the ship sealed itself again. She plucked at his tunic, walking in circles several times before curling up next to his flattened spine plates. Her body began to put out a slight vibration, the rumbling sound soothing his nerves. Kittens were quickly becoming his favorite Earth lifeforms. Aside from Amy, anyway.

Dorn piloted the ship out of the hangar bay. The *Reckoning* was so close, it filled the holoscreen that showed the shard's surroundings the moment he was clear of *Outreach.* If Cygnian vessels were undoubtedly beautiful, Sadirian ships were downright ugly. Weapons bristled from every surface of the huge warship. The metal was somewhere between slate gray and beige and the overall shape blocky and unnatural. A surge of pity swept through him as he thought of the Sadirians doomed to live out their existence in such places.

Behind him, *Outreach* loomed like a bright beacon. He centered his view on it briefly, taking in the spiraling shape of the coils surrounding its central spire, its smooth lines and plentiful viewports. It was even more beautiful within, with plants and other natural features softening the interior. The overall spacious design promoted a sense of wellbeing.

Dorn sent a quick broadcast to the *Reckoning* requesting permission to board and was immediately approved. At least the Sadirians were being helpful, now that they had nowhere else to go in the galaxy. Another surge of pity flooded him as he thought of how the war with the Tau Centauran Assembly had decimated their people and their homes.

Perhaps it was time for the Cygnians to relinquish their neutrality. Dorn would speak with Kral when he had a chance. They needed to take a stand—to stand with Earth and her allies, even if those allies had abused their power in the past. Dorn and his people needed to be looking forward.

He flew his shard into the hangar bay the Sadirian soldier directed him to, circling to a clear area among the masses of ships within. Huge, circular Interceptors, sleek black skimmers, and clunky shuttles filled the bay. Dorn's ship was a gem gleaming among them.

The hatch for his shard would open toward the ground, becoming a ramp that he could slide down, twisting around and leaping to his feet when he landed. The tiny life form still purring on his back would probably not like that. Though it chafed his warrior's pride, he let himself slide down the ramp on his stomach, landing on all fours on the hangar's floor. He looked over his shoulder to see the kitten stand, stretching her legs and back while letting out a huge yawn.

"Did you enjoy the trip?" he asked.

Queenie's lips pulled in a smile. "I did, thank you." She leapt to the floor and stretched again, then took off between the ships. "Come on, Cygnian. I haven't got all day."

Dorn laughed and shook his head as he followed.

Chapter Seventeen

Just outside the hangar bay, Queenie came to an abrupt stop. She spun around and sat facing Dorn, her ears pressed against her head, then began forcefully licking a paw. Dorn looked past her to see the Commander of the *Reckoning* approach. The Sadirian's brow was furrowed as he stared at the kitten, his lips pulled in an uncharacteristic frown.

Dorn was glad for it. Marq was one of the Sadirians whose emotions had been suppressed by their High Council in an effort to make them more effective soldiers. The very idea made Dorn's spine plates rise and his claws push forth from his fingertips. Better to frown and to feel than to always wear the placid expression of the emotionless near-automatons that they had been.

Striding past the kitten, Dorn forced a smile to his face. Marq slowed, his eyes narrowing as he glanced around surreptitiously. A twinge of guilt filtered through Dorn's hearts. The Cygnians had not been kind to Marq and his people, even though they were obviously trying to change their ways to improve life for all in the Coalition.

"Dorn," Marq said. "We are honored by your

presence."

"Confused and curious as well, I would think." Dorn extended his arm in greeting.

The Sadirian's eyebrows rose, but then he smiled and gripped Dorn's arm just below his elbow. Dorn did the same and went so far as to rest his other hand on Marq's shoulder for a moment. As he stared into Marq's eyes, Dorn couldn't help but wonder if he was truly who he seemed to be. Dean would have had enough time to return to the *Reckoning*. He could be masquerading as anyone. Still, Dorn would rather be mistaken and show the Scorpiian kindness than perpetuate the mistrust his people had shown him. It was time for them all to move forward together.

"What brings you to the *Reckoning*?" Marq asked, releasing Dorn's arm.

Dorn scrambled for an explanation that was plausible. With his concerns about Marq's identity, it didn't seem safe to share their mission.

Dorn looked down at Queenie and said, "Someone wanted to visit her old home."

Marq's frown returned. "I see."

"Is that a problem?" Dorn asked, genuinely confused by Marq's seeming disapproval.

Marq took a deep breath and opened his mouth, as if he was about to launch into a lengthy explanation. Instead, he snapped his mouth shut, then sighed.

"It might be," Queenie said, her voice high and strained, yet with a tone imperious enough that Queen Ehmach herself would take note. "If everyone aboard the ship is still mad at me."

"For what?" Dorn arched an eyebrow. How could the crew be mad at a kitten?

Queenie set both paws very precisely on the ground and looked away, her ears plastered back against her skull. "For incapacitating them when I tried to take over the ship."

Dorn wanted to laugh. He desperately wanted to laugh. But the way Marq stiffened and the way Queenie was reacting… She wasn't joking. Neither of them were.

"You…" Dorn said. "Tried to take over the ship?"

She turned to him then, glaring through narrowed eyes. A shiver passed through his spine plates.

"And very nearly succeeded," she said.

"How?" The word came out a bit choked at the end. Dorn had never had a very high opinion of Sadirians, but the idea that the crew of their best warship could be taken out by a kitten was absolutely ludicrous.

Queenie looked away again. "Dean helped me." Her voice took on a sad cast as she went on. "I thought he was my friend."

That explained… Well, nothing really. Except to further Dorn's understanding of the dynamic between Queenie and Dean. To think that the Scorpiian had stooped to using a kitten for his ends. Dorn's antipathy for Dean rose to new levels.

"And afterwards, you had us all carted away to the space station," Queenie said. "Right when we became able to communicate with you. Now Patches and Bandit have found their own people, their own families, while mother and I are in exile. She's not even a space cat, just a normal, ordinary Earth cat. She's supposed to be your pet, and pets are family!"

Marq took a step closer. "It isn't exile, it's to keep you safe. I visit as often as I can."

"You visit your wife," Queenie snapped.

"And you, too," he said. "You all went to the station for your safety. Dean can reach you here. *Outreach* was built by the Vegans. They're constantly watching for Scorpiians."

Queenie snorted. "Well, I have news for you, *Grandpa* —"

Dorn jumped in before Queenie could give away more than he was ready to share. "They're doing their absolute best to keep your kittens safe."

Queenie's glare intensified, but she picked up on his desire to keep their secrets for the time being.

"Yes," she said, her voice mockingly sweet. "Their absolute best."

"I'm so sorry, Queenie," Marq said quietly. "I didn't know."

"Know what?" She stood, her tail twitching in the air as she stormed toward him. "That I had my own plans for my life that didn't include sitting around in your chambers with stupid toys waiting for you to stop by and pet me? That I was intelligent and willful enough to take action?"

Marq lifted one arm, then dropped it to his side. "I didn't know that you needed me."

Queenie blinked a few times, and she cocked her head to the side. She quickly looked away, only glancing at Marq from the corners of her eyes, but Dorn could see the way her fur bristled, the uncertainty on her furry little face.

"If I had known what you needed, I would have been more attentive," Marq said. "Emotions are new to me, but I love you as much as I love your mother. I'm sorry I didn't make that clear. I'm sorry I wasn't there for you."

"I…" Queenie stared at him for a few moments, at a loss for words. Then she let out a little chuffing sound. She walked over to Marq, weaving in and out around his ankles. She glanced up at him and said, "Well, I'm glad you're finally admitting it, at least."

Marq smiled as he stooped to pick her up. She purred loudly, rubbing her face on Marq's chin. Dorn's hearts gave a little tug, warmth filling him at witnessing such a happy moment for Queenie. She caught him smiling, then pushed away from Marq, reaching her paws toward Dorn. He gave Marq an apologetic look as he took her.

Marq shrugged, still smiling at Queenie. "It's more

than I ever thought I'd get."

Chuckling, Dorn placed Queenie on his shoulder. She dug her claws into his tunic to keep her place, still purring.

"We do need to get back to *Outreach* eventually," Dorn said. "And sooner rather than later. I'll see that she gets safely home."

"You do that." Marq's stare hardened till it actually held a hint of menace, further lifting him in Dorn's esteem. It was obvious how much he cared for Queenie. With a wave, Marq headed down the corridor and was quickly out of sight.

"It's that way." Queenie pawed at the air, indicating the direction she wanted him to go. They continued that way for a few minutes, heading upward through the ship.

By Dorn's sense, they were getting close to the upper hull. He jerked to a stop as Queenie somehow managed to climb down his body head-first, claws caught in the fabric of his apparel. When she was close to his knees, she leapt to the floor, then scurried toward the opening for a maintenance tunnel. Dorn's apprehension grew as he stared at the narrow, closed hatch.

Many of the Coalition's soldiers were considered what Sadirians called 'glitches'—genetically engineered specimens that didn't turn out as planned. In most of those cases, they were much larger than anticipated. The previous Sadirian rulers had been more concerned with efficiency and compactness when designing their citizens so that they could make their ships and stations as small as possible and save on resources. Dorn's lip curled up at the thought. The *Reckoning* was designed for larger Sadirians —the ones considered mistakes—but these maintenance panels and tunnels were still meant for humanoids who were on average a foot shorter than Dorn. He wasn't looking forward to squeezing through the space.

Queenie made several impressive leaps up to the access panel, swiping her paws across it in a complex pattern. The door slid open, revealing a narrow corridor. Dorn would have to turn sideways and duck a bit to fit through. He would be vulnerable to attack, to traps. He wouldn't be able to maneuver or fight. As he tried to figure out the best way to proceed, Queenie darted forward.

"Queenie!"

She ignored his call, disappearing around a corner. There was nothing to do but follow. He had to keep her safe. He curled down and twisted diagonally so that he fit into the tight space, hurrying after her. Conduits ran parallel to the floor, covering most of the surface of the tunnel on either side of him—even above. The *Reckoning* might be built for bigger soldiers, but it had still been designed to use every millimeter of space as efficiently as possible. The lighting was dimmer in the maintenance corridor, allowing him to see a deeper spectrum. Energy hummed along the wires hidden beneath the metal next to him.

When he reached the corner where Queenie had turned, he carefully glanced around its edge. The fluffy kitten was waiting at another cross tunnel. As soon as she saw him, she darted forward again. Dorn let out an exasperated sigh. He glanced at his surroundings, his hearts pounding as he thought of all the scenarios that could end very poorly for him. Still, he couldn't let Queenie go forward alone.

"What's taking you so long?" Queenie's small voice called out to him.

He found her sitting in the middle of the next corridor staring at him expectantly. Something was off about the conduits that crossed the wall next to her. To his right, he felt the thrum of energy moving through the ship. To the left, there was a curious gap, the flow seeming to be rerouted to the ceiling and beneath the floor. Dorn leaned closer, scrutinizing the metal of the conduits, but couldn't see any breaks in them.

"This is it." Queenie climbed up the wall using the conduit like a ladder. She lifted her paw and pressed it against a completely nondescript section of pipe.

Mechanisms hummed to life behind the metal. An outline of light appeared in the shape of a small hatch at waist level that Dorn would barely be able to crawl through. The hatch shifted back and then slid into the wall. Queenie leapt through the opening, then turned to face him.

"Hurry up," she said. "It doesn't stay open for long."

His hearts felt as if they had moved up to his throat, their pounding beat making his skin tingle. If he wasn't careful, Amy would pick up on his nervousness. She might try to come and help him, endangering their plan. Swallowing his misgivings, Dorn leapt through the opening, catching himself with his hands on the other side and rolling up to his feet. Queenie wove around his ankles as soon as he stood.

"Impressive," Queenie said. "You should find an excuse to do that in front of Amy. It might make her think more highly of you."

"What—" He let out an exasperated sigh, choosing to let the matter go rather than react to the kitten's baiting.

Pale gray walls like the ones in the maintenance tunnel seemed to press in on his sides. The ceiling and floor were a bit darker, making the short corridor seem even smaller. The hatch slid shut behind him. He turned to look at it, noting how it blended in from this side as well, though the outline of the hatch was visible from here. Aside from the lack of conduits running along the walls, the corridor was identical to the ones they had just traversed.

This area was not some add-on to the ship. It had obviously been created along with the rest of it. But that meant the High Council would have been aware of it. There was no way they would have let this much space within one of their warships be left unused. Dorn recalled hearing that Dean had been one of their operatives before they fell. Just how much power and access had the High Council given him without anyone else knowing?

"Come on." Queenie trotted down the hallway, her tail held high and a spring in her step. He couldn't remember seeing her look so happy.

She raised her paw at the end of the corridor where a small access panel rested several inches from the ground. Unlike the larger one above it, this one was mounted on top of the wall, as if it had been added after the ship's construction. It was the perfect height for her to stand on her back legs and press her paw to. A conduit—the only one Dorn could see in this section—ran from the makeshift panel to the larger one properly embedded in the wall above.

"Dean put this in for me," Queenie said. "He knew I was smart even before I could talk."

"Did he?" Dorn's stomach was churning, his senses poised and alert. He had no idea what awaited them on the other side of the door, but was beginning to suspect that Queenie at least would be safer than he originally thought. Was it possible the Scorpiian actually cared for the kitten?

"Well, he figured it out quickly," Queenie said. "He opened the door one day, and I was staring up at him from right here." She giggled, the translation accompanied by a chittering meow. "You should have seen the look on his face."

Dorn hoped Queenie didn't look up at his face at the

moment. He was having trouble schooling his expression and was uncertain what she'd see there. The door slid open, shifting his focus to his other set of worries. Queenie darted into the chamber.

"Come on," she said, excitedly.

Dorn followed with much more caution. The room beyond was worse than he'd imagined. Built with the sparse decor of the Coalition and their ever-present desire to cram as much as they could into as little space as possible, he found himself standing in the middle of a small, circular room, with only one other exit visible. It was a large hatch directly across from him with enough reinforcements to make him wonder if it opened straight into space. About four feet off the ground, worktables were built into the walls wherever they would fit. Storage cabinets lined the space beneath, their transparent doors giving him glimpses of bizarre tools and containers of odd fluids, unidentifiable floating clumps, and even glowing material.

Three stasis tanks lined the walls, the chrome covers of the floor-to-ceiling cylinders obscuring whatever—or whoever—was inside. Unlike the standard Sadirian regen beds, which kept soldiers in stasis while they were healed during sleep, these looked more like their escape pods. There was no aim for comfort in their design, and they were each barely big enough to hold one of the larger Sadirians Dorn had seen. They were so compact, he could pick one up and wrap his arms around it if he wanted to.

But what had Dorn's hearts racing and his spine plates on end was the tank in front of him. It was clear-walled for some reason and twice the size of the others. It had to be bigger to make room for the assorted apparatuses that lined the sides and back of the cylinder. At least a dozen mechanical arms rested against the sides of the tank, each ending with pinchers, syringes, drills, clamps, or other devices he didn't even have a name for. Dorn's stomach cramped, his muscles tightening with dread as he imagined Buddy or one of Dean's other victims suspended inside.

"Maker." Dorn's voice was rough when he tried to speak. "What is this?"

Why would Dean torture people? With the amount of resources he obviously had access to, he could use the Coalition's mental programming pods to get any information he needed directly from their minds. He could use the same technology to implant memories into the people he replicated so there would be no gaps in their timelines. Perhaps he had replicated a scientist or engineer from *Outreach* and managed to infiltrate and alter the station's scanners so that he was undetectable.

Queenie followed Dorn's gaze, her shoulders slumping and her head dropping close to the floor. Her ears lowered, and she seemed to collapse in on herself. Dorn prayed to the goddess that she had never seen Dean using the main tank. She skulked over to Dorn, pressing herself against his boot.

"That's Dean's chamber," she said, her voice smaller than Dorn had ever heard it. "For his improvements."

Improvements? Was he experimenting on people? Dorn's spine plates began to vibrate, his claws were aching to rend something limb from limb—preferably the Scorpiian.

"How could he use this on people?" Dorn asked the question more of the universe than anyone else, but Queenie was there with answers.

"Oh no, he never used it on others. This one is only for Dean. It's his… What did he call it? His growth chamber. Where he would get stronger and faster and smarter so he could complete his assignments."

"Dean… spent time in there himself?" Dorn's words came out breathless.

"I saw him in it once." Queenie slowly walked forward, transfixed. "Right before he found out I could speak. I couldn't hear him, but I could see him. The chamber was… doing things to him. Awful things. He was screaming."

Dorn's stomach threatened to rebel. His hearts pounded and his skin crawled. Queenie curled herself up into a tiny ball, her tail wrapped tight around her paws and her back arched. The fur all along her spine stood on end, like her own form of spine plates. Her wide gold eyes stared at the tank with a haunted quality.

"When the door opened, he fell to the ground," she said. "He was sweating quicksilver, but it was the wrong color. Purplish and glowing. When he saw me, he smiled, but I could tell he was still in pain. He was gasping for breath, could barely move at all, but he reached out to me and smiled. He told me it was going to be okay and that no one could see what he was with the special lights anymore." A mournful growl underscored her words. "The chamber had made him better."

Dorn's muscles flexed, his spine plates ramrod straight. He needed to fight something. Needed to do something. But his target wasn't here. His target…

He stared at the ground, imagining the Scorpiian—his enemy, the one who threatened his soulmate and her family—suffering, yet reaching out to comfort this small kitten. Why would Dean do that? He hadn't even known how intelligent Queenie was at that point. What did he have to gain?

Dorn reached down to pick Queenie up, wanting to offer comfort of his own. When his fingers brushed against her, she leapt straight into the air, fur sticking out all over her body. She landed sideways, back arched and ears flat as she hissed at him, facing him down like a threat. When she saw it was him, she shook her head, her fur lowering, though she kept her distance.

"I didn't mean to startle you," Dorn said.

"Forget it," she said. Her ears were still pressed firmly

back against her skull. "If Buddy is here, he'll be in one of these other tanks. We need to find him quickly. Before Dean returns."

Chapter Eighteen

Queenie ran to the stasis chamber to their left and stood on her back feet, resting her front paws against it. After a few seconds, the top half of the chamber shimmered, then became transparent. Dean had given the kitten unprecedented access. Dorn wondered if it was because he didn't know of her intelligence or because… Because he actually considered Queenie a friend.

Dorn's hearts had never felt such conflict. Dean was his enemy. The threat he posed couldn't be ignored. At the same time, Dorn had to wonder how Dean could be so cold and ruthless, yet capable of obviously caring for another living being. Dorn looked down at the kitten who had stolen her way into his own hearts as well, watching as she leapt back and craned her neck to look at the contents of the tank. It was empty.

"Not that one," she said. "Maybe here."

She ran to another tank and did the same thing, pressing her paws against the tank until the top half became transparent. A man was inside. Dorn's hearts beat faster as he hurried over, peering at the occupant. The man had sandy brown hair, a strong jaw, and laugh lines that were visible even in stasis. His silver uniform made Dorn think he must be a Sadirian soldier assigned to the *Reckoning*. Queenie confirmed his suspicion as soon as she ran to the center of the room again, far enough from the tank that she could see inside.

"Oh." Her voice was filled with disappointment. "That's Len. He's in charge of the ship's science division."

The science division? That was a high rank among Coalition ships. He would have access to the entire ship, as well as the supplies on board. Dorn glanced back at the strange containers in the cabinets beneath the worktable, but his attention was drawn to the large tank in the center. Perhaps that was how Dean obtained whatever supplies he needed for his… alterations.

"Maybe this one." Queenie ran to the third stasis tank.

Dorn's hearts felt as if they had frozen. If Buddy wasn't here, Dorn had no idea where to look next. The chrome of the cylinder flickered, revealing a man with short, dark hair, a crooked nose from a bad break that had healed wrong, a jaw covered in stubble, and arms thoroughly decorated in tattoos visible from beneath the sleeves of his Earth-style T-shirt. Dorn blew out a breath, his head dropping forward as his tension faded.

"What?" Queenie asked. "What is it?" She ran to the center of the room, her eyes widening when she saw that it was Buddy inside the tank. "We found him! We found him!" She started spinning in circles, leaping up excitedly as she spoke.

"We did." Dorn smiled at her, then picked her up, cradling her against his chest in a gentle hug. "I couldn't have done it without you. Thank you."

"Amy will be so happy." Queenie purred loudly, the soothing vibration easing more of his tension.

He laughed. "She will indeed. Now we just need to get him and Len out of here."

Each tank had a control panel next to it. The design looked typically Sadirian. Dorn activated the panel for the tank holding Buddy, searching for the release button. Instead, the panel's controls flashed red, a loud warning klaxon beating against his ears. He held Queenie closer, crouching and scanning the room for threats. He activated his wristbands' shield function, increasing power to protect the kitten from danger. As long as he held her close, she would be within his wristbands' protection.

"Oh no," Queenie said. "I know that sound from safety drills. It's the ship's self-destruct."

Dorn felt as though his veins were flooded with ice. How could he have been so foolish? The design of the chamber might be Sadirian, but this space belonged to a Scorpiian. No Scorpiian would leave their base unguarded, and their favorite traps were those that used DNA as a trigger. He turned back to the panel for Buddy's tank, selecting a different control. The cylinder shimmered to chrome again, hissing sounds accompanying its ascent into the ceiling. A cycling thrum built above them, and then the tank shot away. A panel closed behind it and blocked their view of whether it truly made it from the ship. Dorn prayed for the Maker to watch over them all.

"What are you doing?" Queenie asked.

"Ejecting them." Dorn hurried to Len's tank and activated the same command. He watched as it rose into the ceiling. "It'll get them clear of the ship." He hoped.

"What about everyone else?" Queenie's body trembled against his chest. "What if the alarm isn't sounding outside of this chamber?"

Shit.

Dorn used the vocal controls for his wristbands to activate a communications channel with the ship. Marq answered the transmission, his voice strained and a loud klaxon sounding in the background. Dorn had no idea a single sound could both reassure and terrify him.

"Tell me this is you and you can stop it," Marq said.

"It was me, but I can't," Dorn said. "Evacuate the ship. If you see your Chief Science Officer, shoot him."

Queenie let out a little hissing gasp, then snuggled closer against Dorn's chest.

"But try not to kill him," Dorn added.

There was only a slight pause before Marq said, "The Scorpiian is on my ship."

"Maybe," Dorn responded.

"This could be a trick to get control of the *Reckoning*."

Marq's voice was a bit out of breath, as if he was running. Raised voices sounded around him, followed by Marq ordering people to get to escape pods. Dorn was grateful that Marq was complying with Dorn's instructions, even if he had doubts. "Dean could be trying to get us all off the ship to take it over."

"I don't think so," Dorn said. "We found his hidden base of operations and triggered a failsafe trap. He won't want to leave any evidence behind." At least, Dorn wouldn't.

"Alright. Wait, Queenie…" Marq's voice hitched up a notch, the calm facade breaking. "You have to get her off the ship."

"That's my next priority," Dorn said. "Just take care of yourself and your people."

"Understood." Marq ended the transmission.

"What are we going to do?" Queenie said. "The alarm only lasts a few minutes. We'll never get to an escape pod in time."

Dorn rushed to the empty tank, gauging its size against his frame. There was no way he could cram himself inside, but Queenie would have plenty of room.

He smiled down at her and said, "What are you talking about? There's one right here."

Queenie craned her neck to look at it. Her eyes were wide when she turned back to him.

"You won't fit." She shook her head. "We have to find

—”

“We have to get you to safety.” Dorn activated the command to open the tank, then started pulling the kitten away from his chest. She dug her claws into his tunic.

“No!” she yelled. “I’m staying with you.”

They didn’t have time to argue. Dorn pushed out one of his own claws and used it to slice through the laces running up the front of his tunic. He pulled it off of his torso, the kitten still clinging to the material.

“Use those claws to keep yourself tethered to the padding in the pod,” he said. “I’ll be right with you, holding onto your tank. My wristbands have atmospheric generators in addition to shielding. I can survive in space for quite a while.”

He hoped, anyway. The charge in his wristbands didn’t last forever.

“Dorn…” Tears glistened in her golden eyes as she looked at him, her pupils huge.

“I’ll stay with you, I promise,” he said. “I swear to keep you safe, little one.”

“But who will keep *you* safe?”

He chuckled, setting her inside the bottom of the tank. “I have Amy for that.”

He stepped back as the door to the cylinder slid shut, then activated the control to eject it, watching as it rose up through the ceiling. There was a protrusion on the bottom that he could use as a handle and from what he’d seen with the other pods, he wouldn't be crushed when the door to the escape tube closed as long as he curled himself up beneath the pod. He clamped his spine plates tight against his back, clasped the handle in one hand, and closed his eyes, praying to the Maker that his grip would hold.

"Come on, come on." Amy paced in the command center, alternating between chewing on her thumbnail and her lower lip. Both felt bruised and she had started tasting the metallic tang of blood. She hugged herself with one arm, staring at the holodisplay as if she could make the schematics for the *Reckoning* give over their secrets.

What glimpses she could get of Dorn's emotions were not reassuring in the least—nor was the fact that she could feel him shielding them from her. They were supposed to be partners. What was he experiencing that he was so intent on keeping from her?

One of the Vegan's holodisplays began to emit an alarming beeping noise. Amy had learned the names of the Vegans in the command center. They were easy to remember, with them all being based on the colors outlining the black stripes along their backs.

Millie, short for Vermilion, called out, "Sir?"

Cerulean hurried over, Amy at his heels. The Vegans spoke in their sibilant language, poking at the screen as different shapes and colors flew across it in patterns whose meaning she couldn't work out.

"What's going on?" Amy asked.

Cerulean looked at her with wide eyes. If he were human, she would say his expression read as a mix of concern and pity. He nodded at Millie, who immediately flew into a flurry of action. Alarms began to blare on the station.

"What is going on?" Amy demanded.

Cerulean ignored her—or rather, kept his focus on Millie.

"Bring up the *Reckoning* on the main holoprojection unit," Cerulean said, clasping his hands behind his back. "Notify the Life Ship, and prepare to mobilize all available rescue units."

"Rescue units?" Amy hurried to stand beside him, her stomach flipping like she was in free-fall on a roller coaster with a broken safety bar. Her cheeks prickled as if they were covered with needles, and her brain was being crushed in her skull by the fear pounding through her. She took a deep breath, pushing aside the panic, centering herself, and said, "Cerulean—"

He cut her off with a curt wave of his hand. Amy was considering picking him up and tossing him across the room or shaking him till he gave her the answers she needed. Millie's emerald scales had paled to lime green, making the red outlining her black stripes stand out in vivid contrast. Millie cleared her throat and let out a squeak, then tried again.

"Sufficient distance has been attained to raise station shields between the *Reckoning* and *Outreach*," Millie said.

"Deactivate repulser beam and raise shields," Cerulean said.

"Shields?" Amy stared at the hologram, which was now filled with a view of the *Reckoning*.

It was much farther away. A flicker of light between it and the station was the only clue she had that they were interacting at all. Then a screen of translucent white flashed between them. Tiny little dots started flying out from every part of the warship. Was the ship breaking apart?

"Please, someone tell me those are escape pods." Amy's voice was barely above a whisper, her throat so tight it hurt to breathe.

"They are," Millie said.

Amy took a deep breath, trying to push down her emotions, to bring them under control. The last thing Dorn needed was her panic distracting him from whatever was going on over there.

"Why is the ship being evacuated?" Amy asked.

"The self-destruct sequence has been activated," Cerulean said.

"What?" Amy gasped. "Why?"

"We do not know," he said.

"Can you stop it?" she asked. "Disable the ship's systems?"

"We can not." Cerulean straightened, hands behind his back once more.

Amy's spine felt electrified, her skin covered in pins-and-needles. They had to do something. *She* had to do something. She was desperate to find a way to help Dorn.

"Even on Earth we have ways of disabling ships," she said. "What about an electromagnetic pulse?"

"That would disable all technology, including some that is potentially keeping people alive," Cerulean said. "Anything we do to try to stop the self-destruct risks disabling the escape pods or their life support systems or shielding. It could trigger premature detonation. We must trust that they are doing what needs to be done and give everyone as much time as possible to escape. We will stand by to assist…"

His voice trailed off. Amy didn't need him to finish his sentence. She did it for him.

Survivors.

Her heart was in her throat when she turned back to the screen. She reached out to Dorn, desperate to connect with him, to know that he was okay. That he had found Buddy. A wave of warmth washed through her, taking her breath away. She felt it like a caress, as though Dorn was in the room brushing his knuckles over her cheek.

Her voice broke as she tried to speak, but she managed

to say, “How long?”

The hologram filled with light, so intense it blinded her. The station lurched beneath her feet, its own alarms blaring. Instinctively, she threw up her arms to shield her eyes. Blinking against the burning in her retinas, she forced herself to look back at the projection. A shower of sparks filled the edges of the hologram. The center…

The center was filled with shrapnel and debris. Huge fragments of metal hurtled toward them, the white light of the station’s shields growing brighter as they impacted. The floor lurched again, but not as harshly as before. Some of the metal flying toward them still burned around the edges, though the embers faded quickly in the cold vacuum of space.

Amy clasped her hand to her mouth and shook her head, tears streaming down her cheeks. She took a step closer to the hologram, unable to breathe, unable to think.

Unable to feel Dorn.

Chapter Nineteen

What the hell kind of shitshow was Bron flying into? He angled his shard away from the *Reckoning*, keeping his fighter clear of *Outreach* station's repulser beam. There was no way he wanted to get caught up in that level of Vegan technology.

Why were they using it on the Coalition vessel in the first place? It must have something to do with the strange energy readings he was getting from the warship. Bron hummed a note to bring up a different scan, hoping to gain insight into what was going on, just as the *Reckoning's* energy readings spiked. A nanosecond later, the warship exploded.

"Maker!"

He steered his ship into the shockwave, riding it out past Earth's moon and hoping his cloak would hold. The impact flipped his shard end over end, his small ship's inertial dampeners unable to keep up with the changes in direction and momentum. The lockbox next to him flew around the pilot's compartment, bashing into him. Bron gritted his teeth as it hit his mechanical leg, a blast of feedback flooding his mind with something most Cygnians never felt—pain.

He jerked his leg away from the lockbox, then released the controls and braced himself with his arms and his right leg to keep himself from bouncing around the inside of the ship. Wary of letting the lockbox near the thin fabric of his pantleg again, he used the bottom of his booted foot to pin it to the interior wall. His ship settled into a sideways spin. After what felt like forever, his shard managed to compensate for the changes, bringing the ship into a more stable trajectory.

Bron let out a breath, then reclaimed the controls. He would have to inspect his leg later to see if it had been damaged, though he couldn't imagine the box being able to harm him. The most advanced cyberneticists in the galaxy had assisted him—Queen Ehmach herself negotiating for the 'repairs' to his body after his injury.

The holodisplay flickered, then resumed the view of the space around his ship. Bron felt as though he'd swallowed a gravity well when he took in the scene around him. His shard was floating in a sea of debris. Chunks of metal of all sizes drifted past him, some with wires protruding that still sizzled. His left leg seemed to ache in sympathy—or perhaps it had been damaged more than he realized by the lockbox. Through the field of shrapnel, Bron could see *Outreach* station, uncloaked since it was on the far side of Earth's moon and cleverly located out of sight of any of the primitive planet's mechanical satellites.

What the hell had just happened? And where was Dorn?

A deep feeling of misgiving grew in Bron's gut—what was left of it, anyway. Lights sparked all over the station, small ships were launching and heading in every direction, though most were aimed towards the area where the *Reckoning* had been. More ships appeared from the lunar surface, access ports opening in patterns of dots on many areas of Earth's one natural satellite. Bron's brow lowered over his eyes as he steered his shard deeper into the debris.

"Have we cleared this quadrant?" Amy pointed at a cube of space highlighted in the holographic display before her. They had activated the hologram shortly after… After the *Reckoning* had been destroyed.

Cerulean cast a quick look at her, his lips pulled into a frown. "We are collecting escape pods as quickly as possible."

"I'm not as worried about the people in the pods as those out of them," she said. "Didn't you tell me they should be able to survive for several days in the escape pods but only a few minutes in their uniforms?"

The Vegan let out a deep breath, but nodded. "This is true, however, we do not know whether the explosion damaged the escape pods."

"They still have a better chance than the people outside of them."

Cerulean nodded, then turned to Millie and began speaking in their language. Amy was glad for the reprieve. She picked at her lower lip till it bled, the pain just more static in the sea of despair drowning her. In the recreation of the space just outside the station, cube after cube changed from red to gold or green as rescue crews scanned them for survivors and marked them as clear or needing more attention.

The blue ones worried her disproportionally. She couldn't shake the feeling that Dorn was in one of them. It was probably pessimism. The blue cubes had been deemed most unlikely to have survivors, and were the lowest priority to search. The trajectory of the escape pods also shouldn't have sent anyone there. She had been assured that there were routes programmed into the systems that would take all the ship's escape pods to the cluster of cubes being patrolled by Vegan ships and the few Coalition ships that had survived the destruction—only because they hadn't been on the *Reckoning* when it blew up.

Amy felt sick. Her back was a wall of cramping muscles, the pain almost enough to double her over. Instead, she kept herself absolutely upright, locking the spasming muscles in place. She wouldn't distract anyone from the rescue operation and didn't want to be removed from the command center. She also didn't want to take the time to explain why the pain was keeping her going, giving her hope.

Ever since the *Reckoning* had been destroyed, the pain in her back had been growing. At first, it was a flash of fire that made her cry out. Cerulean had been concerned, but she'd waved him off. Now, the skin and muscles of her back felt stiff, as if they could hardly move at all. She dreaded the thought that it was somehow related to Dorn, to what he was going through, and yet… If she was feeling his pain, that meant he was still alive.

She knew he was. She was sure of it, had to believe. If he wasn't… She bit her lips together so tightly it hurt. How could she care about him so much when they had only just met? How could she love him?

The other half of her soul was out there somewhere. She just had to figure out where he was and reach him in time.

Cerulean suddenly perked up and turned toward her. "Amy, you must go to hangar bay twelve immediately. This drone will show you the way."

He lifted his hand, the nearest silver bands of his exosuit turning into liquid and flowing up from his arm onto his palm. The metal formed what looked like a mechanical bumblebee the size of a golf ball. It rose from his palm and hovered briefly before heading toward the door. Amy couldn't speak. A lump had formed in her throat that she couldn't form words around. Instead, she nodded at Cerulean, then ran after the drone.

Dorn's back was a blanket of misery pounding against his consciousness. He couldn't move. His muscles punished him with crackling pain any time he tried. All he could do was focus on his mission—even though he couldn't quite remember what it was. What he did remember was that he had to hold on. He had to help protect… someone. To stay near them.

His right hand was frozen in place, a tight fist gripping a metal bar, while his left arm surrounded some kind of large metal tube. His chest was plastered to it as he shielded it with his body. He tried to assess his surroundings, to bring his mind back into focus. Something familiar was approaching. *Someone*. There was another he should be reaching out to, but his energy was so low, so fractured.

He opened his eyes to see a giant shard of milky-white crystal rising up beneath him. Or next to him. It was hard to tell in the vastness of space. All around, the distance held stars and darkness. Closer, bits of metal pinged off of the cylinder, the threat to its precious contents making his spine plates rise and vibrate in warning.

Pain tore through his back again. His spine plates were

like lightning rods for it. He grunted, the sound muted within the confines of the thin layer of atmosphere generated by his wristbands. A voice traveled through the molecules giving him breath, more familiar energy washing through him.

"Relax, brother," Bron said. "This time, I've got you."

The shard attached to the cylinder, then turned and began to navigate through the debris, heading toward a large space station. *Outreach*. Dorn's thoughts were becoming more coherent as they approached an open hangar bay.

Outreach was as important as the cylinder. Both held life forms he loved.

Amy!

He reached out to her instinctively, her face filling his mind's eye, her love and terror flooding through him. She was coming to him, desperate to see him. As desperate as he was to see her and hold her—if he could get his body to obey.

The shard landed on the hangar bay floor and shields flickered over the open port behind them. Rays of light bathed his body as the bay was simultaneously decontaminated and pressurized, a hissing sound letting him know he would have more atmosphere available shortly. Bron appeared at Dorn's side, one hand covering his as he helped Dorn finally release his grip on the cylinder.

"Easy, brother," Bron said. "You have healing to do."

"Healing?" Dorn tried to stand, but straightening his back sent more waves of agony pounding through him. He had never felt pain like this before. "Bron. I need to be upright before she sees me."

Bron's brow furrowed in confusion.

"Amy," Dorn said. "She'll worry. I can already feel her fear."

Bron scowled, but struck his wristbands together, activating them. He held them above Dorn's back and said, "You must have been caught near the initial blast. Your muscles have partially crystalized and there is permanent fracturing."

Crystallized? Cygnian bodies did that upon death. But if it was only his back, the Unmaker was not coming for him. Still, Dorn had never heard of a Cygnian being injured so severely that part of their body crystalized.

His prism-mate, Lar, had crystallized almost completely only a few days past, the Unmaker trying to claim him. Lar had fought his way back from it. His soul had returned to his body for his soulmate. Dorn would get through this for Amy. He would hold her again.

"Do what you must," Dorn said.

"It will hurt."

Dorn nodded. "I know."

Bron hummed a note that activated a sonic vibration—a healing technique they had actually learned from Becca and Sophie while they worked to save Lar. Dorn felt his back begin to pulse, the sound waves slowly intensifying. The stiffness was replaced with fire, lines of it crackling all through his skin. He focused on erecting a wall between himself and Amy. She couldn't feel this pain with him. He would never forgive himself if she did. He ground his teeth together as the pain escalated, his vision flooding with white as the crystalline structures in his muscles disintegrated.

The crackling stopped, leaving Dorn's back in throbbing agony. Bron hummed a more familiar note of healing and a wave of cooling energy suffused Dorn's back, numbing most of the pain. After a few moments, Bron deactivated his wristbands, then placed one of his hands on Dorn's chest, helping him to slowly straighten.

"Better?" Bron asked.

Dorn nodded, trying to force a smile. "Much."

Bron didn't smile in return. Dorn could feel a sense of dread still coming from him.

"What is it?" Dorn asked.

"You have scarring." Bron said. "It's most likely permanent."

Dorn shrugged, the movement making him wince as brief lines of fire shot along the surface of his back. He pushed it away, focusing on what needed to be done in the moment. At least the pain faded quickly.

"I'm here and I will heal," he said. "That's all that

matters."

Bron stared at him a moment, then nodded. He turned to the cylinder and said, "You were covering as much of this with your body as you could when I found you. I could barely see the thing. What is so important in here that you risked your life to shield it?"

"Queenie!" Dorn turned to the cylinder, panic flooding him.

He didn't know where the release was to open the escape pod or how much oxygen was left within. He stabbed his claws through the top of it and rent the metal apart. His back burned from the effort, but he ignored the pain lancing through him. The moment there was an opening big enough, the little kitten leapt onto the open edges of the cylinder, then ran up his arm to perch on his shoulder as she rubbed her face forcefully against him.

"You didn't leave me," she said. "You didn't leave."

"I promised I wouldn't," Dorn said, laughing.

Another wave of sensation hit his back. Fear, disbelief, concern, but most of all relief and love. He turned to see Amy standing in the now-open archway that led into the station. One hand was clamped over her mouth, as if she was stifling a scream, and the other tight around her waist. Tears streamed down her cheeks.

"Amy," Dorn whispered.

She shook her head as she ran to him, arms outstretched. At the last moment, Bron stepped between them, grabbing her off her feet with one arm and spinning her around. Immediately, Amy began thrashing against Bron's hold, kicking at his thighs with her feet, ramming her elbows into his torso, and pounding on his arms.

"Put me down, you son of a bitch, or I'll make you regret ever being born!" she roared.

Dorn's eyebrows rose. Maker, his mate was fierce. Bron half-dropped, half-threw her away from him, trying to get himself clear. He held both hands in the air as she started toward him, backing away quickly.

"Just be gentle," Bron said.

"Like hell," Amy spat.

"With him." Bron gestured wildly toward Dorn, retreating from Amy more quickly. "His back was injured in the explosion."

Fear flooded through her again, flowing clearly through their bond. Amy turned back to Dorn, eyes wide.

"I thought you guys were invulnerable," Amy said.

Bron rubbed at his ribs. "Apparently not."

"There are limits to what we can endure," Dorn said.

"But, you'll be okay?" she asked, approaching him slowly.

The tremor in her voice, the fresh trails the tears had left on her cheeks, it was too much. Dorn grasped her around her waist and pulled her to his chest, leaning in for a deep kiss. The softness of her lips was bliss, the only balm he needed for his lingering pain. She threaded her arms around his neck, cautious at first, but then responding with the same passion.

"Ugh, if you two are going to keep being all kissy-face, at least let me down," Queenie yowled.

Dorn broke off the kiss, amazed as he saw Amy wipe another tear from her face. That his fierce warrior mate had cried for him stunned him to his core. He leaned in to claim her lips again, but Queenie squirmed in his grasp.

"I knew it," she yelled, nipping his fingers. "Put me down. Better yet, you there. Pick me up."

Dorn and Amy laughed, turning their heads to watch as Queenie started giving orders to Bron. His brother lifted his hands again and took a step back, his expression somewhere between concerned and baffled.

"Dorn," Queenie snapped. "Get me closer."

Dorn lifted his arm and opened his palm so that Queenie could use it as a springboard. Bron took another step away, but he had only spent time with dogs. He had no idea what a kitten's range was. Queenie lowered the front half of her body and waggled her hips, pupils wide as she stared at Bron

"I'm not sure I'm comfortable with—" Bron gasped as Queenie leapt across the space, landing on his forearm. Bron froze, eyes wide and mouth open as the kitten ran up his arm to his shoulder and sat there. He stood with his arms still held aloft as if he didn't know what to do or how to react. Slowly, he turned to look at the kitten perched imperiously on his shoulder.

"Cats are not like dogs, brother," Dorn said.

"Especially this cat." Amy stepped closer, prompting Bron to stiffen even more, and scratched under Queenie's chin.

The kitten began to purr. Bron's eyes widened further. He cautiously reached up and took over scratching beneath Queenie's chin until the kitten tilted her face, bringing his finger to her cheek. A look of awe washed over his face.

"Yet another remarkable Earth creature," Bron said.

"You'll learn all about her when you're babysitting," Dorn said.

Queenie narrowed one eye as she lifted a paw to Bron's finger and pushed it down. "Excusc mc?"

"After what we've been through, we're family," Dorn said. "If you'll have us. And Bron is my brother."

Queenie looked over at Bron. She batted her eyes and cocked her head to the side. In a tone that dripped with sweetness, she said, "Uncle?"

Amy had been pinching her lips together, but at that she burst out laughing. She wrapped her arms around Dorn's waist, again with great care, and pressed her face to his chest.

"I like the sound of that," Amy said.

The moment the words left her lips, a high, blaring alarm rang through the room. The entire group froze.

"I do *not* like the sound of that," Dorn said.

"What is it now?" Queenie whined.

Cerulean's voice came over the hangar bay's speakers, shouting to be heard above the klaxon. "Amy Myers, report to Station Command immediately."

"That can't be good," she said, nerves flowing out to him through their bond.

"Whatever it is, we'll face it together." Dorn hugged her closer, then reached out and rested a hand on Bron's free shoulder. "As a family."

Bron stared at Dorn's hand, one eyebrow arched, but then he nodded. "Give me a moment to make sure my shard is secure. We don't want anyone poking around in my inventory."

Amy cocked her head, staring at Bron in confusion. Before she could ask anything further, Dorn sent a silent warning to her through their bond, willing her to trust them, to leave it be. The less they spoke of the lockbox, the better. Especially with Dean most likely still on the station—and undetectable.

A tremor ran through Dorn as he remembered the 'growth chamber' in Dean's quarters. The Scorpiian had paid a high price for his concealment. Dorn only hoped that no one else would have to pay for Dean to achieve his goals.

Chapter Twenty

The group ran as quickly as they could toward the command center. As they approached, the main doors opened before them. The drone flying along beside them headed straight for Cerulean. He barely seemed to notice it landing on his shoulder, then being reabsorbed by his exosuit. His attention was intent on the holoprojection in front of him, various areas of the station highlighted. He straightened as Dorn and his group entered.

"*He* wishes to speak with you." Cerulean's lip curled up as he gestured to his right.

Dorn's hearts seemed to freeze as he saw Dean standing off to the side, arms crossed over his chest and brows furrowed in a deep scowl. After a moment when time seemed to stop, rage slammed into him from Amy, his hearts pounding along with hers, his skin prickling, his back a network of electric impulses that brought his pain spiking back. She lunged toward Dean, but staggered to a stop when she felt Dorn's pain wash through her. Turning back to him, she put one arm around his waist and her hand against his chest.

"He's not really here," Dorn said. "It's a

holoprojection."

"Lucky you." Dean stalked toward them, dark eyes blazing. "What did you do to the *Reckoning*?"

"The question is, what did *you* do?" Dorn said. "It was your trap that initiated the self-destruct systems."

"You couldn't have gotten close enough to activate it." Dean sneered as he spoke.

"It was me." Queenie's voice was high and strained, a plaintive meow underlying the translation. "I showed him where you live on the *Reckoning*. Where you *lived*." She lowered her head, ears pressed back against her head.

Dean's eyes widened, and he dropped his arms to his sides as he stared at the kitten. "Why?"

"You shouldn't have taken Buddy," Queenie said. "Or Len. You shouldn't be taking anyone."

A muscle in Dean's jaw began to twitch. He turned to face Dorn.

"I'm done being nice," Dean said. "Give me my lockbox, and I'll deactivate the station's self-destruct."

"What?" Amy gasped. She turned to Cerulean and said, "You can stop him, right?"

Cerulean let out a long hiss, his golden eyes narrowing as he glanced over at Dean briefly before returning his attention to the holodisplay of the station. The spines running along his back stood straighter, his tail lashing back and forth. Dorn had never seen him so agitated.

"We do not know the extent of what the Scorpiian has

done to our systems," Cerulean said. "He seems to have had access for quite some time."

Millie spoke up, her scales a dull lime. "Whenever we disable one aspect of the system, another comes online to override it. I have never seen anything like it."

"I've picked up a few things over the decades," Dean said. "You have five minutes left." He smirked, and added, "Or do you?"

"You piece of shit." Amy lurched forward, but Dorn grabbed her around her waist and held her back.

"Again, hologram," Dorn said.

Bron's eyes widened as Queenie ran down the front of his body as she'd done to Dorn earlier, then leapt to the floor. Bron reached for her, but she was too fast and small. She ran to the hologram of Dean, rearing up on her back legs with her front paws in the air. Rather than attacking, she held her paws as if pleading with him.

"You can't destroy *Outreach* station," she said. Her voice held a plaintive note that tugged at Dorn's hearts. "It's my home."

Dean's frown deepened. "You'll find another one."

"But I like this one," she said. "My whole family is here."

"You have family on Earth, too," Dean said.

"I'm not an Earth cat." Queenie dropped her front paws back to the ground and stomped one. "I'm a space cat. I belong in space, like my brother and sister. If you destroy

Outreach station, too, I'll lose my home."

Dean stared at her for a moment, a muscle in his jaw twitching. He looked away and said, "You'll get used to it."

"But I don't *want* to get used to it." Queenie stomped her paw again.

Dean opened his mouth, but snapped it shut, glaring at the others as if they were intruding on a private moment. Dorn was fairly certain that they were. He grew more confident in his suspicions that the Scorpiian truly cared about the kitten.

"You don't have to do this," Dorn said. "The High Council is gone. There's a place for you here, with us."

Half a dozen gasps sounded in the room as every pair of eyes turned and fixed on him. Even Cerulean turned away from the hologram, a choked hissing coming from deep in his throat as his neck frill began to inflate. Dorn had never seen a Vegan do that. He fought the urge to take a step back.

"Do you know how many Sadirians Dean just killed by destroying the *Reckoning*?" Cerulean said, his voice low and grating. "Have you any idea what losing one of their last warships will do to their people?"

The muscle in Dean's jaw twitched again. He stood straighter, hands clenched into fists at his sides. He stared at the wall as if seeing through it, deep lines forming at the corners of his eyes.

This wasn't right. Dean had a reputation as a mercenary, not as an assassin. Dorn had no doubt the Scorpiian had a body count, but it was tangential, the result of situations he had created for the High Council, not through intentional direct action. Dorn had seen the look on warriors' faces when they made their first kill in battle. He saw it now on Dean's features.

"The High Council designed Dean's chamber on the *Reckoning*," Dorn said, still staring at Dean's face. "They're the ones who included the genetic failsafe. Dean circumvented it for Queenie, so that they could spend time together, but never thought anyone else would find his base. He didn't intend for the *Reckoning* to be destroyed."

The Scorpiian's gaze whipped to Dorn, their eyes locking. Dean's eyes narrowed, a harsh gleam filling them.

"There's a saying on Earth about intentions," Dean said. "And how they can lead to Hell."

Dorn stepped forward. "I've seen your 'growth chamber,' friend. If that isn't a type of hell, I'm grossly misinterpreting my lessons about Earth cultures. I'm offering you a chance out of it."

"I'm not your friend." Dean glanced at Queenie, but quickly looked away. "I have no friends."

"I'm still your friend," Queenie said. "Please, Dean."

Dean stared at the kitten so intently, Dorn wondered for a moment if the Scorpiian might think he could somehow affect her through the hologram. Dorn knew it was possible—had seen it himself when Amy's sister, Sophie, manifested powers she had gained while saving the life of her soulmate, Lar. Dorn wasn't certain what Dean intended, though. He wanted to believe the Scorpiian wouldn't hurt the kitten, but couldn't take that chance.

"Queenie." Dorn stepped forward, stooping down to grab the kitten and pull her away. He cradled her against his chest, staring up at Dean.

Was that a flash of hurt? Disappointment? The expression didn't last long enough for Dorn to be able to tell. But as Dorn stared into Dean's eyes, he knew what he saw in their depths.

Regret.

The Scorpiian looked away, then the holoprojection vanished. A moment later, the alarms stopped.

"What?" Cerulean said, turning back to the holoprojection of the station.

"The self-destruct has been deactivated," Millie said. "The station is safe."

"None of us is safe while the Scorpiian is among us," Cerulean said. "Increase scan intensity to—"

"It won't work," Dorn said. "Dean has… altered himself."

Cerulean's eyes narrowed. "Altered how?"

"I'm not sure." Dorn shrugged. "It was part of his base on the *Reckoning* and that's all been destroyed. But, I do know he was able to alter himself enough that UV light won't reveal him anymore. I doubt other scans will."

"To make such changes would require modifications at a genetic level that can not be achieved in an established life form," Cerulean said. "Modifications of that sort should only be possible before birth."

"But we've been altered—my sisters and I," Amy said. "Dorn told me. Some sort of alien was powerful enough to change us."

"Yes, but the Cygnian Maker is—" Millie stopped speaking abruptly as Cerulean turned toward her, hissing a warning.

What had she been about to say? Dorn knew that the Vegans held knowledge about their goddess that went beyond any of the teachings among his people. He was still adjusting to thinking of the Maker—and the Unmaker—as a single alien entity who was directly involved in their lives. Lar had met her, interacted with her, during the short period of time when he had been so near death that the entire prism considered him beyond help. Thankfully, Sophie and Becca had stubbornly refused to accept that.

Cerulean straightened, his face a mask of calm as he said, "The Cygnian Maker is not the Scorpiian Maker."

"Aliens that powerful…" Amy shook her head. "You should really be keeping tabs on them. How many 'Makers' are running around out there?"

"Too many," Millie murmured.

Every Vegan turned to stare at her, their spines

stiffening along their backs and a low hiss filling the air. Cerulean pulled himself up even taller, hands clasped behind his back, though his tail thrashed wildly behind him as he glared at her. The scales on Millie's cheeks turned bright pink. She very pointedly returned her attention to the small holodisplay at her station, running her hands through the controls.

"We must attend to the urgent matters at hand," Cerulean said. "Our continued rescue operations and addressing any and all areas of station security that the Scorpiian has compromised."

"We need to warn my parents," Amy said. "And find a safer place for them to stay."

"They should move to Harbor," Dorn said. When Amy turned to him, he went on. "It's a town in Kansas that is the main base of operations for Earth's Department of Homeworld Security. You'll have many allies to assist you if needed."

"Queen Ehmach seems to be softening towards the Earthlings after seeing the video of Amy's challenge." Bron smirked at Amy and said, "She was quite impressed with your creativity and viciousness. Now that I've felt them firsthand…" Bron rubbed his ribs again and shook his head. "The video didn't do you justice."

Amy's expression didn't change, but Dorn could feel the wave of pride that flowed out from her.

"She likes that I'm vicious?" Amy said.

"Our people are matriarchal," Bron said. "Primarily because our women are much more vicious than our men. They are more in tune with creation as the bearers of children and have no mercy for those who would endanger life."

"Huh," Amy said. "Well, she should keep in mind that I'm not unique in that. If anyone comes to Earth threatening our families, it won't end well for them."

"And that—among other reasons—is why we're working toward an alliance between Earth and Cygnus-Prime," Dorn said.

"Alliances will be more important than ever going forward, especially for the Coalition." Bron shook his head, and said, "It's bad out there, brother. We should help with the rescue efforts."

Amy grasped Dorn's arm. "But you're injured."

"Not so much that I can't help." He kissed Queenie's head, then handed her to Amy. "Keep Queenie safe. I'll be back as soon as I can, and then we can travel to your parents."

"You're going away?" Queenie looked up with her golden eyes.

"Only for a little while," Dorn said.

"And you can come with us when we go to Earth," Amy quickly added. "You can stay with us for as long as you'd like."

Queenie's pupils dilated. "You want to be my people?"

"Are you kidding?" Amy said. "You're never going to get rid of us. You go where we go. Well, as long as it's safe. You can't go with Dorn on his rescue mission."

"I'm happy to stay right here." Queenie nestled down into Amy's embrace, the soothing lull of her purr warming Dorn's hearts.

He leaned in and kissed Amy, softly at first, then more urgently, taking his time to savor her. Queenie's chuff of displeasure brought him back to the room. When Amy pulled back, she grinned at the kitten, holding her closer to her chest.

"Come back to us *safely*," Amy said. "I should have said that last time as well, but didn't realize I needed to be that specific."

He laughed, and with one final light kiss, turned and walked from the command center with his brother in stride.

Chapter Twenty-One

Dorn set the hundredth box within the shuttle they had borrowed from Harbor. How many possessions did Amy's parents have? He trotted down the ramp to their yard, smiling as he saw Rom carrying their couch across the patchy grass with Amy's mother, Shannon, perched on the cushions. She was letting out peals of laughter.

"Set me down," she said. "You might be able to turn yourselves not-blue, but if the neighbors see you carrying me around like this, they'll know something is up!"

"I'm sorry," Rom shook his head. "My translator is broken. I can't understand a word you're saying."

Dorn was glad to see Rom's playful nature coming out again. Their pilot had been oddly withdrawn lately.

"Then how can you speak perfect English?" Shannon chided.

Rom shook his head. "Mysteries of alien technology."

"You just responded to what I said," Shannon said, laughing again.

Buddy ran out of the house, his brow drawn in worry, as was his new usual since being rescued. He chased after Rom, waving one arm in the air.

"Put that down," Buddy said. "Oh, geez, is that my mom?"

Rom furrowed his brow and said, "Buddy, what are you talking about? That's a couch."

Shannon let out another loud burst of laughter.

"Come on, man." Buddy reached up toward Shannon. "You're making me nervous."

Rom sighed, then set down the couch. Shannon gave Buddy a quick hug, but then squealed as Rom picked her up, tucking her under one arm and starting toward the shuttle again.

"Hey," Buddy yelled.

"I'm supposed to load the shuttle," Rom responded.

"Dude, put her down." Buddy pointed at his father, David. "My dad's right there. That's his wife."

"You're right." Rom nodded soberly. "They should stay together." Rom walked over and picked up David as well so that he had a parent under each of his long arms. Both of the Earthlings were laughing too hard to protest, so Rom simply headed for the shuttle, leaving Buddy behind with his hands on his head, staring at the sky.

Bron passed by carrying a stack of boxes. He paused, stared at Buddy for a moment, then shook his head and set the boxes on the couch. Once they were balanced to Bron's liking, he picked the whole thing up and carried it to the shuttle.

A sense of peace flowed through Dorn, watching his

family working and playing together. This is what his future would hold. Time with his soulmate and her family, time with the warrior brothers of his prism, and time with Bron, his brother by blood. Already, they were mending the rift that had grown between them over the years.

Buddy looked over and caught Dorn observing him. The Earthling scowled and marched in Dorn's direction. Amy stepped between them, appearing from the side of the shuttle.

"I thought you went to get sandwiches," she said, crossing her arms.

"I'm working on it," Buddy said. "I just need to have a word with Dorn first. We haven't had a chance to talk since you and he… you know." Buddy's cheeks reddened.

Amy lifted her eyebrows, a playful energy of her own infusing their bond. "Since what? Since we got married or —"

"Don't even say it," Buddy said.

Queenie bounded out of the shuttle, running past them and yelling, "Since they got all kissy-face!" then darted into the house, giggling.

Buddy sighed and shook his head. "I'm just gonna have a word with my boy, okay?" He gestured to Dorn, circling around Amy well out of her range of attack.

"Don't take him seriously, Dorn." Amy shouted before walking back into the house.

Rom and their still-laughing mom and smiling dad

followed, along with Bron, who was mumbling something about inefficiencies. They all disappeared into the house, leaving Buddy and Dorn alone.

"What can I do for you?" Dorn asked, smiling down at Buddy and draping an arm over his friend's shoulders. "Do you need help running to your restaurant to make those sandwiches we were promised?"

"No, no," he said, resting one hand on Dorn's back and patting his stomach with the other as he looked up at him. "I've got Nika for that."

Dorn looked around. "Where *is* your lovely bondmate?"

"Like I said, she's helping me get sandwiches." Buddy's scowl turned to a smile as his face and body relaxed. He turned his face up to Dorn as his eyes turned silver.

Dorn's hearts began to pound and his mouth went dry. A shockwave of fear ripped through him, too quickly for him to try to hide it from Amy. She appeared in the door, eyes wide with concern, which quickly turned to confusion as she saw the pair together. The silver covering Buddy's eyes—*Dean's* eyes—flowed to the edges of his sclera, leaving them looking human once more.

"Everything okay out here?" Amy asked, taking another step forward.

Dorn had to keep her from approaching. He needed to assess the threat before introducing any new variables.

With a deep breath, he forced his hearts to calm, burying his fear as deep as he could. Behind him, Dean's hand… squirmed. Dorn felt something sharp drag along the striations in his back, tapping against the weaker grooves left behind from the *Reckoning* exploding.

Dorn definitely did not need to be introducing new variables.

"Dorn and I are just having a chat," Dean said. "Big brother to new brother-in-law."

"I don't think he likes the topic," Amy said, crossing her arms over her chest.

"It's fine, Amy," Dorn said. "Buddy is just…"

"Puttin' the fear of God into him." Dean smiled at Dorn and patted his chest with the hand in front of them—a Cygnian gesture he had picked up during his time with the prism. The cadence of Dean's speech, his voice, everything was a perfect imitation of Buddy. "Which is my right as your big brother."

Amy didn't seem convinced. Dorn smiled, trying to send reassurance through their bond.

"Buddy has quite the imagination," Dorn said. "Some of the consequences he's mentioned are… unnerving."

Amy snorted and shook her head. "Well ease up, would you, Buddy? I'm trying to get work done in here."

"You got it." Dean hugged Dorn closer, giving him a shake.

With one last look over her shoulder, Amy went back

inside. The pair stood a few moments in silence before Dean spoke again.

"You gotta relax, man," Dean said, slapping Dorn's cheek lightly. "We're just two pals shooting the breeze, you know?"

Dorn pushed down another wave of anxiety. He didn't want Amy to come back out, wasn't sure what Dean would do. What he wanted.

"Here's the deal," Dean said. "We're gonna make that trade, but things are a little different now."

"I can't give you the lockbox," Dorn said.

He and Bron had returned it to the *Arrow* when Dorn needed more in-depth treatment for his injuries, not that there was much their medic, Nuar, could do for him. Dean leaned in closer, the gesture so like Buddy that it sent a shiver through Dorn.

"I don't give a shit about the lockbox anymore," Dean said. "It's a simple trade this time. Your girls for mine."

Had Dean kidnapped someone else? Becca and Sophie were safely with the others aboard the *Arrow*. There was no way Dean could get to them, with the soul bonds between prism members and their soulmates. Every member of the prism could sense each other's soul, as well as those of the soulmates among them. It was the one reassurance they had that Dean couldn't appear disguised as one of them. A false reassurance.

Had Dean found Hayley? Dorn had a feeling Dean

would not want to trade her, though. The Scorpiian had an edge about him where she was concerned that made Dorn think he'd want to keep her.

Unable to solve that puzzle, Dorn turned his attention to the other part of the equation. Who did Dean consider his girl that Dorn had 'to trade?' He couldn't mean Hayley. Dorn didn't have her. The only girl that left was…

Queenie.

Dorn's stomach flooded with ice. He pushed aside the fear as quickly as he could. It was easier, knowing that Dean would keep Queenie safe—as much as he could, living a wandering mercenary's life. Dorn's hearts sank, sadness weighing them down. It would be Queenie's choice whether to go with Dean or to stay. Dorn wouldn't decide that for her, and he wasn't entirely certain she would choose himself and Amy.

"If Queenie wants to go with you, I won't stop her," Dorn said.

Dean scowled, then slapped Dorn's face a little less lightly. "Don't be stupid, man," he said. "That's no kind of life for a kitten."

He glared at Dorn, an intense purpose filling his steel-gray eyes. The irises turned silver again, the quicksilver flowing over the entire surface.

"So, you're going to give her what I can't," Dean said, his voice becoming low and dangerous. "A family. A home. Safety."

Dorn noticed he left out 'love.' At this point, he had no doubt that was the one thing the Scorpiian *could* give her.

"I will," Dorn said. "Of course, I will."

Dorn would do that anyway. But, Dean considered this a trade. What was the Scorpiian giving in return?

"Good man." He smiled, his eyes returning to Buddy's appearance as he stared at the house. "Moving is smart. Harbor is a better place for everyone. It'll be safer there. But you know, *your* girls, they like to wander. They won't stay behind the walls. You can run into all kinds of unsavory types out there. Have all kinds of accidents."

"Dean—" Dorn began, but the Scorpiian grabbed his jaw, holding it shut with a strength beyond anything Buddy could manage. Stronger than a Cygnian, even.

"Don't. Be. Stupid." Dean bit out each word before letting Dorn go. "We're just two pals. Hanging out." He looked back over the yard and shrugged. "I gotta go get those sandwiches ready. Mom gets really cranky when she's hungry, and Amy turns into a handful even you can't manage." He smiled and laughed, patting Dorn's chest again.

Dorn's stomach churned to hear Dean speak so familiarly of the Myers family. He leaned in again, not quite looking at Dorn—an odd affectation Buddy sometimes had when he was trying to make a point.

"Before I go, let me spell it out for you, since you seem a little clueless," Dean chided. "I'm not coming after the

Myers sisters anymore. Me and my crew. Everyone under my command—and there are more than you think. Lots more. We'll all stay away. You and your girls get to be all cozied up and safe with your soulmates. Everyone else, now they're fair game. But at least those three, I don't touch."

Dorn's mind was reeling. The idea of Amy and her sisters safe… He wanted that, especially from Dean. But could he trust the Scorpiian's word?

"You take care of my girl… and I leave yours alone." Dean tightened his grip on Dorn's back, the pressure sending pain lancing through his scars. "If I ever check in and see Queenie unhappy or—God forbid—hurt, I'm gonna take it out of your hide. And then I'm gonna take it out of Amy's. Then her sisters'." Dean shrugged. "Maybe even their mom and dad's." He laughed, and said, "Hell, I might even go after their neighbors. Imagine that. Me on a rampage." He gave a little mock-shiver, then leaned closer and whispered, "The possibilities are endless."

"I won't let anything happen to Queenie," Dorn said. "Never, if it's in my power to protect her."

"Good man." Dean tapped Dorn's chest once more, then released him and stepped away. He stared down the street, where Nika's truck had just come into view. "Here I come with those sandwiches. I better go."

Dean turned and headed toward the tree line behind the property, hands in his pockets. Dorn took a step after him, then another.

"Wait," he called out.

Dean turned around, still walking backwards toward the trees.

"I meant what I said before," Dorn said. "You could have a place here."

Dean laughed, shaking his head in a gesture that was so like Buddy it sent a chill through Dorn's hearts. Dean scratched his temple, then tapped on it with his forefinger and shook his head.

"Yeah," he said. "Not very bright at all."

He turned and vanished into the trees.

A few moments later, Amy appeared at Dorn's side. She ran her hand along his arm.

"Buddy and Nika are back, in case you're hungry," she said. "I think they might have been here longer than we thought." He sensed her confusion, no doubt wondering how Buddy could have been here talking to Dorn while also getting the sandwiches with Nika.

Dorn turned to Amy and pulled her into his arms, holding her close, feeling her warmth against him. After a while, she pushed back from him, just enough to stare up into his eyes.

"What's wrong?" she asked.

He didn't know where to begin, just that he had to tell her everything. They would face this together, as they would face all challenges. He brushed a lock of hair back from her forehead, then said, “We need to talk.”

Epilogue

Harbor was about to get a bunch of new residents. Olivia went through her to-do list while walking her Newfoundland, Zorro, to the newest housing development on the outskirts of town near the starport. Her brother was the mayor, and he had a laundry list of tasks he needed help with. The Antareans had done an amazing job building a row of new houses all along 'Cygnian Lane,' but it was up to Nancy and herself to work with the new residents so they could make those houses homes.

Not that shopping for anything they wanted for absolutely no cost wasn't going to be the most fun ever, especially since she'd be doing so with one of her best friends. Even better, one of the houses was slated for the third member of their bestie group, Lian, who was the first Earthling to land herself a Cygnian soulmate.

Olivia had missed Lian so much and was thrilled at the thought of her returning to Harbor and spending more time there. Maybe if she had an inviting home, she'd visit more often. Olivia couldn't wait to hear more stories of how Lian's spine had lit up like fireworks when she and Nuar met, how they couldn't keep their hands off each other even still. It sounded like a fairy tale, that kind of love. If it had been Nancy, Olivia would think she was exaggerating the effect of the soulmate bond, but Lian was one of the most down to Earth people Olivia knew.

She laughed at the turn of phrase. Lian hadn't been back on Earth for weeks. She was cruising around the solar system with a bunch of hot blue aliens, having the adventure of a lifetime. Olivia was content to stay in her library, living her own adventures among the pages. She had seen way too many scary sci-fi movies to want to explore outer space.

Still, she couldn't help but wonder what it would be like to love someone like that. To be loved so completely. She could almost imagine a prickling up her spine, just as Lian had described, the sensation spreading over Olivia's back, then down along her arms and legs, pooling in her belly like— Olivia stopped, one hand on her abdomen and her eyes wide. This wasn't her imagination.

She lifted her face to the sky as a cargo shuttle flew above, heading for the starport. Her breath came in gasps as the prickling along her spine intensified, the skin on her back rising in gooseflesh. She felt a tug, as if something was pulling her out of her body, toward the ship. She was flooded with energy, with *need*.

Zorro turned and whined, bumping against her. Olivia was so unsteady, the nudge from the huge black dog knocked her right on her rump.

"Ow." The sudden pain in her bottom brought her back to her senses. She shook herself, gripping Zorro's neck as he licked her and whined even more, as if apologizing for forgetting how big he was.

"It's okay, boy," she said. "It wasn't your fault."

She looked back to the sky, her heart racing, her mind trying to tell her that what she had felt hadn't been real, couldn't be real. But she knew the truth in her heart.

Whoever was in that shuttle was her soulmate.

—

Thank you so much for reading *Dorn: A Scifi Alien Warriors Romance*! The adventures will continue in book five in the *Cygnian 7* series, *Bron: A Scifi Alien Warriors Romance!* Bron is the only cybernetically enhanced Cygnian. As you can imagine, he has extra sympathy for the Tau Ceti cyborgs who have been genetically modified by Norem on the Ceres base. Bron is going to have to reach out for help from an all-new alien species never seen before in the Homeworld universe! And you know that Dean isn't done with everyone yet. This one has some of the biggest plot twists of the series, so look forward to it!

While you wait, I thought you might like a peek at an earlier appearance by Dean. He's always had an interest in cats, but Queenie taught him to truly appreciate them.

Check out this excerpt from *The Department of Homeworld Security* book 14, *Rate of Return.*

Rate of Return

The Department of Homeworld Security
Book Fourteen

Chapter One

This was not a reunion he was looking forward to.

The last time Serac had encountered—what was he calling himself now? Dean—Serac had vowed it would be the last. Yet here he was, standing in an open field near a small dwelling on a primitive planet in the middle of the night. Waiting.

His *zyln,* the elemental spirit living within him, was preoccupied with the dwelling. Something about it unsettled them both.

Serac eyed the entrance, which was situated a few feet above the ground on a wooden porch. On the second level of the building, there was a row of dark windows, one of which kept drawing his attention.

He could easily leap onto the porch's roof and pry open the window to get inside. But why did he want to?

Footsteps crunched in the snow behind him. Serac turned to see a tall, thin humanoid. At least, that was the form Dean was borrowing. Serac was one of the few people who had actually seen a Scorpiian in his natural form and lived to tell about it.

"I wasn't sure you'd come." Dean's voice was lighter in this form. Smoother.

For the moment, Dean's light brown hair stuck up in unruly waves. He was dressed in some sort of uniform with matching dark pants and a jacket over a deep blue shirt that was unbuttoned at the throat.

If that was the garb that people in this small settlement wore, Serac would stand out. He was wearing jeans and a T-shirt, as well as a thicker jacket that was almost unbearably warm.

The air was crisp and cool around him. In other circumstances, he'd strip naked, shift his form, and run through the woods to enjoy the coolness of the ecosystem. His *zyln* rumbled approval deep within.

This place reminded him of Centaurus-10.

It reminded him of home.

"Go ahead," Dean said, nodding toward a particularly tall drift of snow. "Weather patterns in this area are highly variable. You might not have another chance to enjoy this sort of environment. Unless, of course, you've decided to join me."

Serac wasn't ready to confront or commit, so he said, "That's an interesting form you're borrowing. It almost looks Sadirian."

Dean shrugged one shoulder. "It doesn't really make a difference what you want to call this form. Earthlings and Sadirians are genetically almost identical, unlike you Centaurans, who only *look* Sadirian. Well, sometimes."

Serac felt his hackles rise, the hair on the back of his neck standing on end. Dean was baiting him. But Serac wasn't the impulsive thug he used to be.

"You said you'd found a prize," Serac said.

"I have."

"Convince me of its worth. You have three minutes."

Dean smirked and even chuckled. "So in charge. And here I'd heard that you were bowing to a *Lyrian* lately." Dean's lip curled as he said the word. "When you and I worked together, you bowed to no one."

Except my conscience—and even that took too long.

"Two minutes left," Serac said.

"Fine. I've encountered a life form on this planet that seems completely harmless. They're small, furred, with four legs—like most Earth wildlife. The humans call them cats. The Earthlings think they've domesticated them."

"You don't agree."

"No," Dean said. "At best, the cats allow humans to

cohabitate with them. They're extraordinary creatures. I was attacked by half a dozen of them recently. They were harboring a toxin in their claws and bite that required almost an hour in a purification chamber for my body to purge."

For Dean to have needed so much time in the healing chamber, the toxin had to have been particularly problematic for his physiology.

"So, what?" Serac said. "You've called me here to intimidate them for you? Maybe rough them up a little?"

"I plan to capture some," Dean said.

"And you need me for that."

"Need? No." A muscle in Dean's jaw flexed and his smirk disappeared. "I'm providing you with an opportunity. Don't be so stupid that you can't see it."

A growl built low in Serac's throat. He forced it down.

"These creatures are valuable enough that a Sadirian was trying to harvest a DNA sample from them for the Coalition's scientists," Dean said.

Serac snorted. "Sadirians will take DNA from anything. They're obsessive about collecting it."

"True, but this Sadirian was working with a Vegan."

That prompted a quick intake of breath that Serac couldn't quite hide. Dean's smirk returned.

"I thought that might catch your attention," Dean said.

Serac had heard rumors that the Vegans had made an appearance during the Battle of Sadr-4. He'd dismissed it as propaganda from the Coalition of Planets in its effort to maintain their control over most of the sentients in the galaxy.

It had to be a lie meant to scare everyone into staying within their rule. Their High Council had been obliterated and their entire home system destroyed.

Serac clenched his fists as he thought of his people's role in that. The air around him grew colder.

"Vegans are a myth," he said.

"Believe what you will. But know that the DNA of these Earth cats is a high prize—as are the creatures themselves."

"If you want their DNA, why not get it yourself?" Serac asked. "You must have had some available, given that they bit you."

"The samples were tainted by my body's immune response." Dean went on, his voice rising with excitement. "These creatures are unlike anything you've ever encountered. Some of them seem docile while others are outright murderous. And they can switch from one state to the next without giving any sign to their change in temperament."

"Sounds like you have much in common," Serac said.

Dean snorted. "I'm willing to let our past remain in the past. Together, we can capture these animals and market them as vicious guardian beasts. Imagine if we, too, could win their favor and then provide them as pets throughout the galaxy? One moment, the beast is calmly resting upon its beloved owner's lap. The next, it's sprung to attack. We can modify its natural microbiome to make its bite and scratch even more dangerous."

"These all sound like stories for the hearth fires," Serac said.

Dean scowled. "I am not plying you with children's tales. Vegans are real. Cats are real."

"Then capture one and sell it. You don't need me."

"If it were that simple, I wouldn't have called you in the first place. We need someone who understands them. Someone who can control them and teach us how to induce their docile state. And I've found the perfect Earthling to help us. She just needs some convincing."

Dean was talking about abducting a sentient. And from what Serac knew of the Scorpiian, he would absolutely go through with his plan.

The hairs on Serac's nape rose again. His *zyln* grew more alert within, the sense of impending danger growing.

"The human who lives in this dwelling runs a place called a 'pet parlor.' Her name is Kimmy and she is a specialist in controlling animals—including cats."

Cygnus-X, he's planning to do this now.

"If we can acquire her, she will enable us to capture the cats and train them," Dean said. "We just need to persuade her to assist us."

Serac knew what Dean had in mind when he spoke of

"persuading" sentients. Serac wouldn't be part of it. And he couldn't let this happen.

"Your plan has one obstacle," he said.

"And what is that?"

Serac's *zyln* rose up in him, energy coursing through his body as it began the change.

"Me."

—

Dorn's book kicks things up to a whole new level. Ripples from the events in this book will definitely be felt in the other series set in this universe. For now, keep an eye out for book five in the *Cygnian 7* series, *Bron: A Scifi Alien Warriors Romance*.

If you want to learn more about Dorn and the other Cygnian warriors' universe, you can check out *The Department of Homeworld Security* adventures. Many of the novellas have been collected in the first two series omnibuses, *The Department of Homeworld Security Omnibus 1* and *The Department of Homeworld Security Omnibus 2*. Or you can pick and choose with the individual novellas. You'll want to check out *Export Duty* to see why Rin is so afraid of cats, and *Nothing to Declare* for the very first appearance of Dean. And don't forget to read *Trade Secrets* to see how Queenie almost took over the *Reckoning!*

I'd love to keep in touch. Join my newsletter at sendfox.com/cassandrachandler to hear about all the adventures happening in Cassland. And if you enjoyed this book, please consider leaving a review at your favorite book review site. I'd really appreciate it—reviews help readers and authors alike!

Thank you for reading *Dorn: A Scifi Alien Warriors Romance!*

Cassandra Chandler

About the Author

USA Today Bestselling author Cassandra Chandler uses her vivid imagination to make the world more interesting, spawning the ideas she turns into her enthralling Science Fiction Romances and darkly evocative Paranormal and Urban Fantasy Romances. Fast-paced and funny, lighthearted or dark, her stories will introduce you to characters you'll fall in love with and worlds you long to explore.

www.ingramcontent.com/pod-product-compliance
Lightning Source LLC
Chambersburg PA
CBHW071257250626
47159CB00004B/1228

* 9 7 8 1 9 4 5 7 0 2 9 3 8 *